LUCINDA FOX

The Mum Swap

Cover photography by Miicha/Bigstock. Cover design by Danijela Mijailovic

Second edition

This book was professionally typeset on Reedsy. Find out more at reedsy.com

Contents

Dedication

To Tabitha, Jemima, Alexa and Seth who remind me daily how tricky growing up can be.

Chapter 1

The paparazzi came out of nowhere. Camera flashes exploded like fireworks all round me. I couldn't see their faces beyond the bursts of light, but suddenly I understood everything. All the pieces just fell into place and landed with a thud in the pit of my stomach. I'd been such an idiot.

I didn't know what to do, so I just ran. I ran down the stairs of the BBC building and into the crowds of people who were busy minding their own business and didn't realise that my life had just totally fallen apart. My eyes were full of tears, and that made it hard to see where I was going. People shouted at me as I barged past, but I didn't care. I didn't care about the snot either, or the fact that I must have looked a real mess. I just kept going. And as I ran, I thought about Lydia and how she'd be waiting at school for news. I thought about Sam and how upset and then angry he'd looked as it dawned on him what was happening. But most of all, as I ran down the busy street towards Regent's Park, I thought about Mum and how on earth I was going to explain to her what I'd done.

But wait. That's how my story ends. I need to begin at the beginning or this whole thing won't make much sense to you. Here are a few basics to get you started. My name is Kitty, and all this happened last summer, when I was twelve. I could spend ages telling you all about me but you'd be bored rigid, so I'll keep it short. I live with my Mum. There are just the two of us (which I think was part of the problem). My dad died when I was four. My best friend is Lydia, who I've known since preschool. And here's the biggie: I'm adopted.

Being adopted might not seem like a massive deal to you, but it caused me no end of problems last summer. It's not like it was a surprise or anything – they told me I was adopted right from the off. I'd never really thought about it, to be honest. It was just the way it was. But then, when things started to get a bit tricky with Mum, I thought about it a lot.

Life started to go fairly spectacularly wrong when the fair came to Woodston, where I live. It comes every year. They always set up on a bit of waste ground round the back of the precinct. I walk past it on my way to school, and each day, it grows as more and more trucks arrive. I love the way the rides are all packed onto the lorries and then open up like flowers, bit by bit, until you can see the whole thing. When I was little, I used to try and guess which ride was which as the fair men slowly pieced them all together.

The best bit, though, is when the rides are all built, the music starts to play, and then you know the fair is really here. It always opens on a Friday night, stays all day Saturday and Sunday, and then they shut everything up, pack it all back onto the lorries and move on to the next place.

Every year, Mum and me would go to the fair together. It was a bit of a family tradition. I'd tell her when the trucks started arriving, and we'd do this countdown thing until Friday when it was all built and ready. Then, on Saturday afternoon, after we'd been to the supermarket and cleaned the flat, we'd walk over there. It wasn't that big, not like a theme park or anything.

There were a few rides that whizzed you up into the air and then back down, some that spun you around, others that did both. They were painted in bright colours with portraits of old film stars stuck on. Elvis and Marilyn Monroe and Danny and Sandy from *Grease*. Some of the pictures were pretty rubbish, to be honest, but you could tell who they were meant to be. There was always music blaring out, and it smelled of popcorn and frying onions and engine oil. I loved it.

Mum would let me go on three rides and try my luck on one stall. That was my limit because we never had much cash to spare, so I had to pick carefully. I'd walk round the whole thing really slowly so that I could see exactly what there was before I made my choice. I always had a go on the hook-a-duck because you won a prize whether you hooked the duck or not. I learned pretty young never to try at the stalls where you have to throw something to win. They're a real rip off. The hoops are too small to go round the blocks, or the dartboard is so hard that the darts just bounce straight back out. But you can't go wrong with hook-a-duck.

Anyway, when I saw the fair starting to arrive last year, I got really excited like I always do, and I told Mum so that she could make sure that she was free to take me. Me and Lydia were buzzing about it too. Each morning on our way to school, we talked about what we were going to go on. I know we sound a bit babyish, but none of the bad stuff had happened to me then. I was still a kid.

Anyway, on the Friday, Lydia came into school with this cocky smile on her face. She was trying to play it cool to start with, but I could tell that something major had happened. I'm her best friend. I know everything about her.

'Guess who's going to the fair on her own?' she said, and

3

she was hopping up and down on one foot because she was so giddy.

'You never are!' I said, my eyes getting wider by the second. 'How come?'

It was a bit of shock, to be honest. It had actually never crossed my mind that you could go to the fair without your mum.

'Mum says it's fine,' Lydia said. 'As long as I stick in a gang and don't go off by myself.'

'Not sure two of us makes a gang,' I said.

'Me neither,' agreed Lydia, but from the way she was grinning, I could tell that this wasn't going to be a problem. 'But Mum's fixed it with Jess and Chloe's mum. We can all go together.'

My heart sank. Chloe and Jess Bell were twins and family friends of Lydia's, but I wasn't that keen on them. They were a bit pleased with themselves for my liking, but I put up with them because Lydia thought they were alright.

'Do you think your Mum will be OK with that?' Lydia asked casually.

She scrutinised my face, trying to work out what I was going to say. I had no idea what Mum would say, to be honest. At that stage I hadn't really asked to do anything on my own.

'Course she will,' I said confidently, but I wasn't quite as sure as I sounded, and a bit of me was sad to be leaving Mum behind. The fair had always been this thing that we did together. Then again, I knew she wasn't really interested and only went because I wanted to go.

So actually, I thought, she would probably be pleased if I went with Lydia because it would mean that she didn't have to. And it would be cheaper too because she'd only pay for rides for me and not both of us. In fact, she might let me have her ride money as well so that I could go on more things. Lydia's mum didn't have the three-ride rule. Lydia just got money from her dad and could spend it on what she wanted.

I was buzzing all day. I couldn't really concentrate in lessons, because I was thinking about what I was going to wear and which rides we'd go on and how cool it would be to be at the fair on our own. I even got in trouble in history because I wasn't listening and I couldn't answer a question. That's not really like me. I'm actually a bit of a geek on the quiet, but let's keep that between ourselves!

Anyway, the afternoon took forever to finish, and when the bell finally went, I raced to meet Lydia at our place by the Year 7 lockers. When I got there, Lydia was already waiting but she was chatting to Chloe and Jess Bell. I was a bit surprised to see them, as this was our special meeting place, but I supposed it didn't really matter, just this once. Lydia told me the plan. We were going to meet in the supermarket car park, near where they put all the broken trolleys, at seven o'clock on Saturday night. I said that would be fine and I would see them there.

I was on my way home when it first crossed my mind that Mum might actually say no. I ran through the arguments in favour in my head just in case I needed them. There was the one about her not having to go. I thought I'd keep the fact that it would be cheaper in reserve, in case she didn't think of it and gave me her money anyway. Also I was going with Lydia, who Mum still quite liked at this stage, and the Bell twins, who Mum knew a bit. It would still be light at seven, so that wasn't a problem. Finally, I thought I could point out that I'd know loads of people there because although Woodston is part of London, it's only a little place really, and everyone knows everyone else.

I got home and let myself in. Mum was still at work. I shouted hello to Mrs Marshall, who lives downstairs, and she shouted hello back, and then I went upstairs to wait for Mum. I thought I'd try some outfits on to see what would look best for the fair. Mum might even let me borrow her new lipstick and the mascara that makes my eyelashes look really long, and I could experiment with the eye shadow that Lydia bought me for my birthday. It was like a tiny paint palette of gorgeous colours, but I'd hardly used it because Mum wouldn't let me wear make-up, except for dressing up.

I can't tell you how excited I was. Every bit of me was fizzing. It was like Christmas and my birthday and going on holiday all rolled up into one enormous ball of buzz.

Mum was a bit late, so I decided to get on with doing my make-up for the night. I'd seen a picture of smoky eyes in a magazine, and it had a 'step by step' photo thing of how to do it, so I had a go. It wasn't as easy as it looked, and I had a bit of trouble smudging it all so it looked properly smoky. My left eye was definitely better than my right, but it wasn't bad for a first attempt. I put on my skinny jeans and my black T-shirt with the sparkly lips. A couple of the sparkles had come off in the wash, but it was still my favourite. By the time I'd finished, I looked pretty fantastic. I was just thinking that it was a shame I didn't have any shoes with heels, when I heard the front door bang and Mum shout hello.

I rushed out to see her. As I got to the lounge, she was just taking off her jacket and her work security lanyard. She looked a bit tired, but she's on her feet all day at work, so it wasn't surprising. I just stood in the doorway waiting for her to turn round and look at me. I wanted to see her face when she saw how great I looked in my 'going to the fair' outfit.

That's when it all started to go wrong. It was obvious the moment she saw me that she didn't like it. I can always tell when I've done something wrong. She cocks her head on one side and her eyebrows disappear behind her fringe. It's her 'disappointed' look.

'Kitty,' she said, and her tone of voice made my heart sink a little bit further. 'What are you wearing? And what have you done to your eyes?'

'It's the smoky eyes look,' I said, trying to sound casual. 'I got it out of a magazine. Do you like it?'

'Well,' she said, 'I think it might be a bit much for you just at the moment, but it's not a bad first attempt.'

She yawned, pushed her dark hair back from her face and started rubbing at her temples.

'Would you be a poppet and make me a nice cup of tea?' she said.

I was relieved. After a bit of a shaky start, it was going OK. I decided I should make the tea for maximum Brownie points whilst she got used to the smoky eyes and then, when she was feeling more chilled, I could tell her about Lydia and the fair plan. As I boiled the kettle and got out Mum's favourite mug, I shouted through to the lounge to ask her about her day, and she asked me about mine. I didn't really say much and I definitely didn't tell her about history. I took the teabag out of the mug, put just the right amount of milk in and carried it really carefully into the lounge so that I didn't spill any of it on the carpet. I put the mug down on a coaster on the coffee table and sat down next to Mum. I took a deep breath.

'Mum?'

'Yes.'

She was looking at the TV listings in the paper.

'You know the fair's here?'

'Yes. You might have mentioned it once or twice!'

This was Mum's attempt at humour.

'Do you want to go tomorrow afternoon like normal?' she asked.

'Yes. Well, I do want to go, but I was wondering ... Lydia and the Bell twins are going tomorrow night, and they wanted to know if I could go with them. Can I?'

'Well, I don't know ...'

She paused and I could tell that she was thinking about it. I held my breath and watched her face carefully. Mum has a kind, soft sort of face with brown eyes that look almost liquid, like a puppy. Of course, we don't look anything alike, with me being adopted, but I wouldn't mind if we did.

'I thought you liked going with me,' she said after a bit.

She sounded a bit disappointed, and a pang of guilt stabbed into my heart. I did like going with her, but I wanted to go with Lydia and the others more.

'But I suppose if you want to go with Lydia and her mum and dad, that would be OK. You're growing up fast, aren't you, Kitty Cat?'

She smiled at me and ruffled my hair. Normally, I would have said something about having been grown up for ages, but I needed Mum to get the plan whilst she was still in this good mood, so I ignored the growing-up bit and carried on.

'Actually, Lydia's mum and dad aren't going. It would just be me and her and Chloe and Jess. We're meeting in the car park near the broken trolleys at seven and then going to the fair together. It's still light quite late now, so when we've been on the rides and stuff, I thought I'd just walk home. I'll be back before nine, I reckon.'

The plan just tumbled out of my mouth, my words all crashing against one another. I needed Mum to have all the details fast before she had a chance to come up with any objections.

It was no good. Mum's smile fell away and her lips disappeared into a tight, thin line.

'Oh, Kitty. Don't be silly,' she said.

She was almost laughing at the idea, at me.

'You can't possibly go to the fair by yourself on a Saturday night. You're far too young.'

'I'm not going by myself,' I said quickly. 'I'm going with Lydia and the Bell twins, and I'm not too young. I'll be thirteen next birthday.'

I could feel myself getting angry, but I had to keep my cool so she'd see how grown up I'd got without her noticing. My cheeks were starting to burn with the effort. Mum just shook her head.

'It's a no, I'm afraid, munchkin. You're all far too young. I don't know what Lydia's parents are thinking, to be honest. If it was Saturday afternoon, then perhaps I could come with you and sit and have a cup of tea whilst you went on the rides with Lydia. But Saturday night at the fair without an adult in sight. That's definitely out. Sweetheart.'

She looked back down at the paper in her lap as if the conversation was over, but as far as I was concerned, we had only just begun.

'Mum. That's so not fair. I am nearly thirteen. I have been to the fair millions of times and everyone else is going.'

'I don't really care what everyone else is doing,' Mum said without looking up.

This was her no-nonsense voice now.

'You're too young and you are not going and that's final.'

The trouble was I was so upset that I decided to ignore the signals and just keep going.

'But we've made the plan now,' I shouted.

'Well, you can just unmake it.'

'But Lydia's allowed to go and she's younger than me. It's not fair.'

Mum sat up very straight, folded her arms tight across her chest and looked me straight in the eye.

'I am very surprised that Lydia is allowed to go. And the Bell twins. I thought their mum had more sense. But that doesn't alter things one iota. You are not going and that's an end to it.'

I should have left it then. I know I should. It would have been better if I'd shut up and walked away until she'd had time to get used to the idea, but I was so cross that I just couldn't help myself.

'I can't believe you're saying this,' I shouted at her. 'All my friends are going to go, and if I'm not allowed, then I'm going to miss out massively and they'll all be talking about it and I won't be able to join in and they'll laugh at me. They already laugh at me because I don't have new clothes and a decent phone …'

I knew I'd gone too far. The anger in Mum's face turned to hurt, but I didn't care. I wanted to hurt her. She was spoiling my life with her ridiculous rules, and I wanted her to know how difficult she was making things for me.

'I am sorry if you think you don't have new clothes or a decent phone.'

Her voice was very calm and her words came out really slowly, one at a time.

'You have no idea how difficult it is to bring you up on my own. I do my best to make sure that you have everything you need, and I'm sorry if you think that I'm not good enough, but I'm afraid that's just the way it is. There is no way you are going to the fair on a Saturday night without an adult. It's non-negotiable. Now, go to your bedroom and take that muck off your face. Tea will be in thirty minutes.'

And then she picked up her paper again.

I was beyond furious now, but I could see that there was no point arguing with her, so I just stood up and stormed out, slamming the lounge door behind me. Then I slammed my bedroom door as well for good measure. Slamming the doors felt good, but as I threw myself on my bed for a good cry, I was a bit sorry that I'd done it. I felt bad that I'd complained about my clothes and my phone too. I did know how hard it was for Mum, bringing me up on her own, and that she was doing her best, but actually, if this was her best, then it wasn't good enough. She had wrecked my plans, and now I was going to look really stupid in front of Lydia and the Bell twins. And I wouldn't get to go to the fair on top of that!

I sat up and looked at myself in the mirror on my wardrobe door. I liked watching myself cry, and this was better than usual because the mascara was running in thick black streaks all down my cheeks. I felt like someone in a film. And just as I was thinking that, the music from the waltzer started playing and wafted in through my open window and set me off again. I threw myself back on the bed, buried my face deep into the pillow and howled.

Chapter 2

I lay on my bed that Saturday night with my bedroom window wide open and listened to the bass beat from the fair thudding out across Woodston. By the time the music stopped at ten o'clock, I wasn't cross with Mum any more. I could even see her point. Well, sort of. I was never allowed out by myself at night unless it was just round the corner to the minimart to get some milk or something. I don't know why I thought it would be any different just because the fair was in town. But it was time that Mum realised I wasn't a baby any more. I was virtually a teenager after all.

But then things got even worse.

On Monday I was dying to see Lydia to find out what had happened. I waited for her at the spot where Fieldview Road joins Church Street, which is where our walks to school meet, but there was no sign of her. I waited until I was late and then I ran to school. I wasn't worried. Lydia sometimes overslept and had to get a lift to school from her mum. As I got to the school gates, the bell for registration was ringing, so I knew we wouldn't be able to catch up with each other until break. Then, as I was turning the corner to go up to my form room, I saw her. She was leaning against the sports hall wall and laughing in this really over-the-top, fake way, which wasn't a bit like her. The Bell twins were standing on either side of her like bodyguards, and they were laughing too. I felt pushed out.

I called out to her.

'Lydia. Hi!'

She turned to see who had shouted, and then, when she saw it was me, I got a big, beamy smile, which made me feel a bit better.

'Kitty. I've got so much to tell you about Saturday night,' she said. 'I went on that mini rollercoaster four times and I swear I was nearly sick, and there was this boy who kept chatting Jess up ...'

As Lydia was speaking, Jess put her fingers to her lips really dramatically to shut her up. Then Jess linked arms with Lydia and started walking away from me towards their form room. They're all in the same form, you see. It's just me that's on my own. Jess was sort of pulling Lydia along, and Lydia had to turn her head right over her shoulder to finish talking to me.

'I'll tell you all about it at break. See you at the usual spot ...'

And she waved her arm above her head to me and then was lost in a mass of Year 10s. I was glad to have seen her, but I didn't like the fact that Jess had pulled her away when we were trying to talk.

I couldn't really concentrate in class that morning. I was worried. Lydia was my best friend, not Jess Bell's. She needed to back right off and find her own best friend.

When the bell went for break, I packed my bag fast so that I could get out quickly and raced to our place against the wire of the tennis courts. Lydia wasn't there, so I waited. After about five minutes, which is a pretty big chunk of break, I saw her walking along with the Bell twins. They had all linked arms in a long chain with Lydia in the middle, and they were all deep in conversation about something. I could tell it was important, because Lydia was screwing up her nose, which is what she always does when she's thinking.

Lydia looked up and saw me waiting. She tried to wave but she couldn't get her arm free, so she sort of lifted her shoulder instead and then struggled to escape from the Bell twins' clutches and ran to me. She gave me a big hug and I hugged her back. I held on to her for a little bit longer than usual just to show the Bells that I could. Then Lydia pulled away and started telling me about Saturday.

'It was such a laugh, Kitty. You should have been there.'

'I know,' I said. 'Mum just wouldn't budge. I can't believe that your mum was fine with you going on your own like that. You're so lucky.'

'Yeah. She was going to some party with dad, so it was Callum. Like he cares where I am.'

Callum is Lydia's older brother. She moans about him but he's alright really. I'd love to have a big brother looking out for me.

'What rides did you go on?' I asked her. 'Did you go on the waltzer?'

The waltzer is my favourite ride. I love the way the man walks between the cars swaying like he's on a ship, and how if you scream, he just spins you faster and faster. Sometimes you go so fast it feels like the car is going to spin right off the waltzer and away into the sky like Dorothy's house in *The Wizard of Oz*.

'Waltzers are for kids.'

This was Chloe Bell, who had wandered over and was standing very close to Lydia. I remembered why I didn't like her as soon as she spoke.

14

'We didn't bother with them, did we, Lyd?' she said in her stupid, nasal voice. She talks like she's got a cold all the time.

Lydia hates being called Lyd. She always has done ever since we were at primary and someone called her 'Tin Lyd' as a joke. I looked at Lydia, waiting for her to correct Chloe, but she didn't. She winced a bit but she didn't say anything.

'We only went on the white-knuckle rides, didn't we, Lyd?' Chloe said, and she winked at Lydia.

I thought this was totally ridiculous. This was Woodston Fair not Thorpe Park! The closest you get to white knuckles is the Wheel of Death, and that doesn't actually move up and down. It just spins round and round so the centrifugal force pins you to the cage. It's fun but it's hardly 'white-knuckle'. I looked at Lydia to see if she was going to say that she actually liked the waltzer, because I know that she does, but she didn't say anything.

'Anyway,' said Jess Bell. 'We had far too many laughs to tell it all. You missed it, Kitty. End of.'

She looked so pleased with herself as she spoke that I almost wanted to slap her.

'And if your mum still treats you like a baby, then you're going to miss out again,' she continued.

I could hear the sneer in her voice and it made me want to slap her.

'We're all going to the cinema on Saturday, aren't we, Lydia? We're going to see *Espresso Dreams* at the multiplex. Wanna come?'

I didn't know what to say. I hated Jess for calling me a baby, but if I pulled her up on it, she might uninvite me. I looked at Lydia and tried to signal to her with my eyes that this was not OK, but if she saw my signal, she ignored it and just carried on talking.

'Yes,' she was saying. 'I asked Mum and she said if your mum can pick us up afterwards, then I can go.'

She'd already made a plan without me, and that really hurt. We always planned stuff out together before we asked our mums.

'But isn't that film a 15?' I said.

It just slipped out before I had chance to think. Lydia and I had watched the trailer for *Espresso Dreams* on YouTube knowing that we'd never get to see it at the cinema, because our mums wouldn't let us go. Or so I thought.

I knew as soon as the words were out of my mouth that it was a mistake. Chloe Bell started sniggering.

'Since when does that matter?' Jess said. 'No one cares if you go to see a 15. They never check your age or anything. Chlo and I do it all the time.'

My cheeks started to burn and I just looked at my feet, hoping that they didn't notice. I felt so stupid.

The rest of break passed with them chatting, me trying to butt in whenever I could and them talking over me. It was really annoying, to be honest, but I thought I'd just ignore them and then talk to Lydia about it when we were on our own. After all, she was my best friend, not theirs.

That wasn't all though. My next problem was how to get Mum to say yes to the cinema plan. I knew I had to tread carefully. Otherwise, it would be the fair disaster all over again. I decided to go for the helpful, reasonable daughter approach.

'Can I go to the cinema with Lydia on Saturday, please?' I said as I was helpfully peeling the potatoes for tea.

I asked as casually as I could so Mum wouldn't think it was a big deal or anything.

'I don't see why not,' she replied. 'If you've done all your homework, of course. What are you going to see?'

Now, this was a tricky question. I could pretend that I didn't know, but Mum would see straight through that one. Then again, if I told her, I was pretty sure she'd know it was a 15 because she had been in the lounge when me and Lydia were watching the trailer. I tried to sound casual, like I wasn't really bothered.

'I'm not sure. I think Lydia said *Espresso Dreams*.'

I waited. I was holding my breath and I just kept peeling potatoes.

'Isn't that rated 15?' asked Mum.

Honestly! You can't get anything past her.

My heart starting to race as I tried to think of how to answer. I couldn't exactly deny the film's rating, but if I didn't, then she was going to say no.

'You know, I'm pretty certain it is,' she continued. 'You girls can't go and see that. Or I suppose you might be able to if you had an adult with you. I'm not sure how these things work. What does Lydia's mum say? Is she going with you?'

I was thinking fast at this point. I didn't want to say that Lydia's mum wasn't going, but I couldn't get over the 15 problem without there being an adult with us. Of course, I could have just lied, but I knew that Mum sometimes spoke to Lydia's mum, so that seemed a bit risky, and anyway, I don't really like lying to Mum. She can usually spot a lie at a hundred paces.

I decided the best course of action was just to pretend that I didn't know and that we would firm up the details later. The main thing was to get Mum to say yes to the idea.

'I don't know,' I said. 'I'll ask Lydia. But if her mum is going, can I go?'

Mum was washing up the chopping board and stuff, and I thought I was home and dry. I picked up the tea towel to show her how thoughtful I could be. But then Mum said, 'Do you know, Kitty, I don't think you can see a 15 film if you're under fifteen, even if an adult is there. I'm pretty certain that's right. It's not a parental guidance thing. I think it's just not allowed.'

I could see the plan escaping and heading for the hills.

'I think it must be fine, Mum, because Lydia, Chloe and Jess are all allowed to go.'

I could tell as soon as the words were out of my mouth that I'd made a mistake. Mum banged the knife down in the washing-up water too hard, and all the water flew up and splashed her top.

'Oh, well, that's alright, then,' she said, but you could tell from her voice that it was anything but. 'If Lydia and Chloe and Jess can go, then it must be fine.'

When Mum uses sarcasm, you know whatever it is must be pretty bad.

'I don't know what's going on with Lydia at the moment,' Mum continued. 'But I'm very surprised that Cheryl is being so lax with her. The Bell twins, I can understand. They've always been a law unto themselves, but I thought Cheryl had more sense. Anyway, I'm afraid you can't go to see a 15 film when you're only twelve.'

She had finished the washing-up and was wiping her hands on the towel in a 'conversation over' kind of way, but I couldn't let it go. This was my life we were talking about. Could she not see how impossible she was making it?

'But, Mum! I have to go,' I said, hoping to appeal to her softer side. 'It was bad enough that you didn't let me go to the fair, but I didn't make a fuss, did I? I just accepted it.'

Mum raised her eyebrows, and I remembered the shouting and the door-slamming, and so I moved quickly on.

'And if I don't go, I'll be missing out again. They'll all be talking about the film for ages, and I won't be able to join in, because I won't have seen it.'

'I don't care, Kitty.'

Mum was using her stern voice again now, and I knew the battle was lost.

'You are too young. These films are rated for a reason, and someone who knows far more about it than you and me has decided that you have to be fifteen to see it. You are twelve. Now, have you got any homework?'

I was so frustrated. I had to make Mum understand what was happening here. If I didn't go to the cinema with Lydia, then the Bell twins would steal her. They had already got their claws into her and they were pushing me out. I would have to fight for her, but how was I supposed to do that if Mum kept stopping me from getting in the ring?

'But, Mum. You have to let me go.'

I was shouting now because I was cross and scared and this was a really, really big deal.

'I have to do no such thing, young lady. You are not going and that's final. I don't want to discuss it any more.'

And that was it. I'd blown it. I knew Mum well enough to know that there was no turning back from this point. Lydia would go to see the film with the Bell twins and I wouldn't be there. Again.

I turned on my heel and ran out of the room. More door-slamming and crying followed.

'I can't understand why you don't just go anyway,' said Lydia the next day when I told her about what Mum had said. 'Tell her that you're at my house. She'll never know that you're not.'

I thought about this for a few moments. Lydia was right. Mum would never ring to check that I was where I said I was. There was no reason to. She trusted me. I was a trustworthy person. So it would be easy to lie about where I was going and get away with it.

But then I thought about how disappointed Mum would be if she ever did find out. I pictured her face, her lovely brown eyes all sad and hurt, and I couldn't do it. I couldn't lie to her.

Well, not just then anyway.

Chapter 3

Problems between me and Mum seemed to come thick and fast after that. I kept asking her if I could do things and she kept blocking me. Lydia and I were still best mates, of course, but it was getting harder and harder to find times when we could be alone together. The Bell twins were always hanging around her and getting in the way.

And I was pretty sure they were bad-mouthing me behind my back. Lydia was strong, but there's only so much of that kind of thing you can stand before the lies start to become a kind of truth. I was desperate to get her away from the Bells so I could make sure that everything was still OK between us, but the more desperate I got, the more Mum seemed determined to wreck everything. It was like she was doing it on purpose.

As a result, there was loads more shouting and door-slamming in our little flat. Well, it was mainly me, to be honest, but I kept getting so frustrated with Mum. I don't know where all the anger came from. One minute I'd be fine and the next it was like someone had flicked a switch inside me. Mum didn't often shout and never slammed doors. Mainly she just looked really sad when I was going off on one, but I was so angry with her that I didn't really care how she felt.

One day, I was letting myself in after school when the door

to the flat downstairs opened, and there stood Mrs Marshall with her cat Merlin in her arms.

'Your mum's not home yet, Kitty. Would you like to come in for a cup of tea and some millionaire's shortbread? I've just made it fresh this afternoon.'

Mum was never home when I got in, so I wasn't sure why Mrs Marshall was mentioning it, but I was hungry and she made fantastic cakes, so I said yes.

I always think it's interesting to go inside Mrs Marshall's flat. It's almost exactly the same shape as ours because it's just below us. But then there are some really different things. Her lounge is where my bedroom is at the front of the house, and our kitchen is her bathroom and kitchen combined, I think. It gets quite tricky to work it out when you are actually in there. I would love to put the two flats side by side and look down on them so that I could compare them properly.

Her flat is really different to ours as well because it's so untidy. Honestly, you wouldn't believe the mess. Sometimes Mum says that it looks like a bomb's gone off in my bedroom, but in comparison to the chaos in Mrs Marshall's flat, my room looks like a palace.

I only ever go in Mrs Marshall's lounge and kitchen. The kitchen isn't too bad. She's always done the washing-up at least. It's not a health hazard or anything, like Serena's house. When I went there for tea once, it was so filthy that I had to tell her I had a weird allergy and couldn't eat anything that my Mum hadn't cooked. Mrs Marshall's wasn't anywhere near as bad as that. There were piles of newspapers and cake tins all over the place, but the sink and the work surfaces were clean. But the lounge! Now that was a different story ...

There was a sofa in there and two armchairs covered in

this sludge-coloured, chunky cord, which wasn't too bad for old-people furniture, but you could only ever sit on the sofa because the chairs always had something else on them. That day, one chair was covered with a massive pile of books that she must have taken off the shelf when she was looking for something and not got round to putting back. The other one had a tray on it with an empty plate, a red spotted teapot and a teaspoon with Buckingham Palace on the end. I could have moved it and put it on the floor, but I didn't want to seem rude. So I sat down on the sofa, which was relatively clear apart from a coat and some folded-up towels that were resting on the back. I sat right at the edge of the seat, near the arm, and made myself as small as I could so that when Mrs Marshall sat down, we wouldn't be sitting on top of each other.

Mrs Marshall had gone off to the kitchen, but she came back quickly with another tray. This one had a plain blue teapot, a tiny striped jug, two mugs with cats on and a plate with five slices of millionaire's shortbread on it.

'Oh dearie me,' said Mrs Marshall as she came in. 'Just look at this mess, Kitty. What must you think of me? Here. Let me move this tray out of your way.'

It wasn't in my way, because I was already sitting down on the sofa, but she gave me the new tray and picked the old one up from the chair and then looked for somewhere to put it down. The wooden coffee table was already piled so high with newspapers and letters that there wasn't a surface flat enough to balance the tray on. There was another table over in the window, but the piles on that one were even higher, so in the end she just sighed and put the old tray back down on the chair. I was left holding the new tray, which was quite heavy with all that stuff on it.

'Oh, this is ridiculous,' said Mrs Marshall when she realised that I had nowhere to put the new tray down. Then she did something that made me laugh. She got her arm and she just swept it over the coffee table, knocking everything that was on it onto the floor. My kind of tidying up!

'There!' she said. 'That's better.'

Then she put the new tray down on the table and stepped over all the stuff on the floor so she could come and sit down next to me. I wanted to giggle really badly. It was hilarious watching her push all that stuff onto the floor like that, but I thought that might be rude, kind of drawing attention to the mess that I was pretending was normal, so I kept my mouth shut and tried not to smile too much.

'Tea?' asked Mrs Marshall, and I nodded, so she poured some into the cup with the Siamese cat on it, splashed in some milk and handed it to me. 'Help yourself to shortbread,' she added.

I did. Mrs Marshall's millionaire's shortbread is to die for. The shortbread on the bottom is crumbly but not so crumbly that it all falls apart when you bite it, and she uses real chocolate on the top and not that cooking chocolate stuff that Mum buys.

'So, how's life, Kitty?' she asked.

She looked at me closely, her eyes narrowing a bit, and nodded, like she was trying to encourage me to open up.

I didn't know what to say. Life was pretty rubbish. Mum was blocking me at every turn, Lydia and the Bell twins were getting closer each day, and I was feeling further and further out of everything. So while I thought about how to answer her, I had a sip of my tea. It wasn't as hot as I expected, and I wondered if it had been made a while.

'Oh, it's OK, thank you, Mrs Marshall,' I said eventually.

I mean, what was she expecting? That I'd tell her it all just like that?

'And school's going well?'

'Yes. Not bad. I got seventy-two per cent in my French test last week. Madame Beaumond was really pleased with me.'

'That's really good, Kitty. You know, school is so important.'

I still didn't know what to say, so I just nodded my head and bit into my shortbread. The sticky caramel bit oozed between my teeth and I tried to lick it off with my tongue. It really was delicious.

'And it'll be your birthday soon, won't it? Thirteen. A teenager. Goodness. It doesn't seem two minutes since you and your Mum moved in upstairs. I remember when I was thirteen ...'

I must have pulled a disbelieving sort of face without realising, because she interrupted herself.

'I know! Hard to imagine, isn't it, but I do. We didn't have teenagers in those days. They hadn't been invented, but I remember that I had a little tea party for me and my best friend Joyce, and my mother made Battenberg cake, which was my favourite.'

I had no idea what Battenberg cake was, but if she remembered it after all this time, then it must have been tasty.

'I think it's hard being nearly thirteen,' she continued. 'Not quite a grown-up but no longer a child exactly. I imagine things get really frustrating sometimes.'

'Yes,' I said.

I could see which way this was going.

'All those things that you want to do but you can't, because you're not quite old enough.'

'Yes,' I said again, but I was starting to get a bit cross. 'It's just like that,' I continued. 'Mum doesn't seem to get it, but it's so hard when all your friends can do things and you can't. They think that I'm a baby because my mum always says no when theirs say yes. Soon they'll just stop inviting me to stuff. I mean, what's the point? I can never go anyway.'

I surprised myself with my little outburst, and so I had another sip of my tea whilst I waited to see what she'd say next.

Mrs Marshall just sat still and looked at me. Merlin had hopped up onto her lap. She ran her hands all the way from his ears to the tip of his slinky tail and he purred loudly.

'Your mum just wants what's best for you, you know? You're all she's got since your dad died, and she wants to keep you safe and make sure that you don't get into harm's way.'

'I know that,' I said. 'But she doesn't let me do anything. I'm growing up. She has to let me out sometimes. She can't keep me trapped in my bedroom like some kind of princess in a tower.'

Actually, I was very far from being kept locked in a tower, but it was something that Jess Bell had said, and I liked the idea of waiting to be rescued.

'No,' said Mrs Marshall. 'I can see how it might feel a bit like that, but you have to remember how very difficult it is for your mum. She is trying to bring you up all by herself. She has no one to share the burden of that with. And when you get to your age, the changes come thick and fast. I know. I remember when my two were teenagers. That was a rollercoaster ride and no mistake.'

Her eyes flicked over to the mantelpiece, where at one end, behind some books and yet another pile of letters, was a double frame with pictures of a man and a woman in it. These were Anthony and Angela, Mrs Marshall's children, who were grown up now and lived somewhere else.

'But you'll come through it,' she continued, looking back to me. 'You just need a bit of give and take. Your mum is doing her best to do the right thing for you, and you perhaps need to think about how difficult it is for her. There's been a lot of door-slamming recently.'

She looked at me in a knowing kind of way. It suddenly struck me that she must hear all of it, my shouting and stamping and door-slamming. I had never thought about her sitting down here listening before, and I felt a blush rising up my neck. I didn't know what to say, so I just kept eating.

'It's a tricky age, to be sure. But I'm sure you'll find a way through. The main thing is that you keep talking to each other.'

I nodded and a crumb of shortbread fell into my lap. I was starting to feel a bit awkward. What was it to do with Mrs Marshall? True, it seemed that she had to put up with my noise. I would try and slam the doors more quietly in future so that she wasn't sitting there knowing our business. But really, what else did it have to do with her? This was between me and Mum and no one else.

I could feel that anger bubbling up inside me again, and I knew I had to get out before I was rude to her. I put my mug down on the carpet next to the sofa and stood up. I must have done it quite quickly, because Merlin jumped and his tail went like a bottlebrush.

'Well, thank you for the tea and the millionaire's shortbread, Mrs Marshall,' I said as politely as I could, but my words came out more harshly than I meant them to. 'I have some homework that I need to do, so I think I'd better go home now. I'll see myself out. Thank you.'

I negotiated my way through the mess on the floor, trying not to stand on anything that wasn't carpet, picked up my school bag and headed up the stairs to our flat. Mrs Marshall didn't follow me, but I could feel her eyes staring after me until I was safe inside with the door shut.

Chapter 4

The next day was Friday, and Lydia was coming round after school. She often did that or I'd go to hers. We'd catch up on what had been happening and swap gossip about people. Mum said she didn't know what we could possibly find to talk about when we'd been together all day at school, but Lydia and I never ran out of things to say to each other.

We were in my room, just lying on the bed and having a laugh. It felt great to have her all to myself without the Bell twins sticking their oar in every five minutes. We had walked out of school after the last bell with our arms linked and our noses in the air, and I really hoped that Chloe and Jess were watching so they could see what proper best friends look like.

Anyway, back at home I'd made us some toast, and we were nibbling it and trying not to make any crumbs because Mum doesn't like me eating in my bedroom.

'How's your Mum been this week?' Lydia asked.

I could tell she was treading really carefully. It's all very well for me to have a go at my Mum, but I don't like it if anyone else does it, not even Lydia.

'Not too bad,' I said. 'She's fine when I'm not actually trying to do anything! It's when I make a plan that it goes wrong and we fall out. I can sort of understand where she's coming from though.'

Lydia looked at me like I'd gone mad, screwing her face up as if she couldn't get what I was saying.

'I mean, it's just me and her, isn't it?' I continued. 'Mum's bound to be a bit over-protective. She's got to make all the decisions about me by herself, and as I'm the oldest, she's had no one else to practise on. And I'm the youngest too, so she's bound to baby me a bit.'

I'd been thinking quite a lot about what Mrs Marshall had said to me, and I could hear her voice in my head as I spoke. *Your mum is doing her best for you. Perhaps you need to think how difficult it is for her.*

'Well, that's all very well,' said Lydia, cutting through my thoughts. 'But she is going to have to let you grow up some time. You can't spend your whole life cooped up in this bedroom, living with your 'behind the times' mum and that mad old bat downstairs.'

I winced a bit at that. Lydia could be quite hurtful sometimes. I know she didn't mean to be, but I found it hard when she was nasty about Mum and Mrs Marshall. She was right though. I did have to find some way of getting Mum to see that I was old enough to be going out and about by myself. I needed to show her that I was virtually a young adult and responsible enough to be trusted. Then she could stop worrying about me so much.

'She needs someone to talk to,' Lydia continued. 'She needs to know what normal thirteen-year-olds are allowed to do.'

I nodded in agreement. Lydia was spot on. Mum was just a bit at sea when it came to parenting a teenager.

'You should get an instruction manual with a baby,' I said. 'They could give it to you in hospital so you knew what you were doing from the start. Age One – learn to walk. Age Two – learn to talk. Age Thirteen – allowed to go out with their mates without World War III blowing up in the living room.'

We laughed at this and spent a while thinking of things that could go in the manual. Age Thirteen – have ears pierced. Lydia already had hers done – twice! – but Mum said I had to wait until I was sixteen. I didn't really mind that at the time, but now, with everything else that was going on, it just seemed like something else that I wasn't allowed to do. Age Thirteen – wear foundation. Age Thirteen – have high heels.

We were laughing so hard that we couldn't breathe, and tears were rolling down our cheeks. It was so funny! Mum popped her head around the door to see what was going on, but we couldn't stop laughing long enough to explain. I saw her look disapprovingly at the toast plate but she didn't say anything, just picked it up and shut the door behind her as she left.

After a while we calmed down a bit. The 'instruction manual' idea had been hilarious, but it also highlighted what the real problem was. I was about to hit the age when other girls could do all this stuff, and my Mum was just stopping it all from happening. And the worrying thing was I could only see it getting worse. Mum wasn't going to change her ideas overnight just because I was changing. Before I knew it, I'd be sixteen and still trapped in the flat with no freedom. And no friends.

'Perhaps we could get her together with my mum and they could have a chat about stuff?' Lydia suggested.

I wasn't sure this was a great plan. Mum and Lydia's mum had always been nice enough to each other, but I didn't think they were ever going to be real friends, and Mum had actually said some quite mean stuff about Lydia's mum after the fair debacle. Obviously, I couldn't tell Lydia that.

31

'I'm not sure that's a great idea,' I said. Then, because Lydia looked a bit hurt, I added, 'Well, my Mum's mad ideas might rub off on your mum, and then you'd be stuck too.'

I could see Lydia turning this over in her head.

'Yes. You're right,' she agreed. 'That wouldn't get us anywhere.'

Even though she was nice about it, I knew that Lydia thought that Mum was being totally unreasonable most of the time.

'No. We need to find someone else to help her,' I said. 'After all, she's trying to do the job of two people, what with my dad not being around and everything.'

And then it hit me, like a horse galloping straight at me at a hundred miles an hour. My stupendous idea! It was so brilliant that it sort of knocked me over and I fell back and stared up at the ceiling whilst I thought about it some more.

'What's up?' Lydia asked, and she dropped back too so we were lying side by side on my little bed and looking up at the ceiling.

'I've just had the most amazing idea,' I said, although then I went quiet because I was worried that if I said my plan out loud, I would see that it wasn't that amazing after all.

'Well?' said Lydia impatiently after a few moments of me not saying anything. 'What is this earth-shattering plan?'

'Perhaps I should try and find my birth mother and get her to help out?'

It didn't sound that bonkers to me. I might not have a dad but I did have another mother. Somewhere. My birth mother. She'd had it easy for nearly thirteen years, but now perhaps it was her turn to step up and help out. And as she was my real mum – well, my biological mum – she would want to do things to make me happy. She had a lot of catching up to do, and surely, to make up for that, she would be glad to be involved and help me out?

I paused for a few moments as I breathed in the words that were flying around the room over our heads. For once, Lydia was quiet too. She just lay there and waited to see what I was going to say next.

'I mean, all this time, I haven't only had one parent. I've had two … well, three really, although I'm not that bothered about my birth dad. So I was thinking …'

I paused for a moment, biting my lip as I worked out what I was actually thinking, but it did suddenly feel very straightforward.

'If I could find my birth mother, then perhaps she could help Mum make some decent decisions instead of the rubbish ones she's been making lately.'

Lydia still didn't say anything but I could tell she was thinking my idea through. Usually she's the one that gets totally carried away about stuff, so I was a bit thrown by her being that quiet. After what felt like forever of her saying nothing, I couldn't bear it any longer, and so I rolled over onto my stomach, no mean feat on such a narrow bed, and poked her on her arm.

'Well?' I asked impatiently. 'What do you think?'

Lydia turned over too so we were lying propped up on our elbows with our heads turned, almost nose to nose. She looked at me and then she was grinning like she'd just won the lottery.

'I think it's a brilliant idea,' she said, her voice squeaky with excitement. 'I can't believe we didn't think of it before. That would solve everything. Your mum will have someone to turn to for help and she won't feel so alone. And your birth mum might be able to help with the money side of things too.'

My insides squirmed a bit when she said this, and I could feel my cheeks going pink. We never really talked about money, but Lydia knew that we didn't have much spare, which was why I couldn't have all the stuff that her dad bought her. She was right though. I hadn't even thought about that.

'Perhaps I could go and stay with her sometimes. I bet she lives in London somewhere. She might be just down the road. She might be someone that I see every day without even realising that she's my mum.'

My mind was racing ahead of my mouth with all the amazing spin-offs from my new idea. And then suddenly all the potential pitfalls began to land on me one by one, like enormous, sloppy snowballs being dropped from a great height.

She had given me away, this woman. She had not wanted me when I was a baby. What on earth would make her want me now that I was nearly a teenager and a bit of a pain in the backside? What if I found her and she agreed with everything that Mum said and I had to battle against two of them and not just one? What if she was even stricter than Mum? Lydia was still talking but I'd stopped listening. I was just thinking about what might go wrong. But do you know, never once during that whole adventure did I stop and think about how Mum might feel if I found my birth mother.

Chapter 5

I spent a lot of time thinking that weekend. I told Mum that I was doing my homework, but I was actually just lying on my bed mulling things over. Sometimes the whole finding-my-birth-mother thing seemed like the best idea I'd ever had, and I couldn't believe that it had taken me so long to come up with it. Then I'd hear a little voice in my head telling me how stupid I was being. How would I even find her name, let alone where she lived? And what if I did find her? She might not want to have anything to do with me.

She had given me away after all, so she couldn't have thought that much of me. What if she had loads of other children that she hadn't given away? Where would I fit in a ready-made family? Then again, that would mean that I had half-brothers and -sisters, and that thought got me all excited again. Round and round it went in my head like a toy train on a track.

By the time it got to Sunday, my plan was feeling like a good idea more often than a bad one. So now I needed to work out what to do next. Mum had never said anything about my birth mother and certainly never told me her name, but I reckoned that it must be in the flat somewhere. There would be a letter or something, surely?

It took me a while to realise that I must have a birth certificate.

I remembered a TV programme that me and Mum had watched where this actress had gone in search of her family history. That's when it dawned on me that I must have one too and that it might have the name of my birth mother on it. Genius!

I knew exactly where it would be too. Mum had this black box file where she kept all the important documents. I knew our passports were there because I'd seen her putting them away after we went to Spain that time. The file was full of loads of other papers but I hadn't paid it any attention, because it looked dead boring at the time, but now I was sure that it would hold the key to finding my birth mother.

In my head I didn't know what to call my birth mother. I obviously couldn't call her Mum, and 'birth mother' was such a mouthful. I started just thinking of her as 'her' or 'she'. At least when I found my birth certificate, I could give her a name.

The trouble was I wasn't totally sure where the box file would be. It was a small flat. There weren't that many places, but I couldn't go snooping about when Mum was in or she'd want to know what I was up to, and even though my plan was only half-formed, there was one thing I was certain of. I must not tell Mum. Secrecy was the key.

So I waited. It took ages, but eventually Mum said she had some bits and pieces that she needed to pick up from the shops, and did I want to come? Obviously, I said no. No sooner was Mum out of the door and down the stairs than I was in her bedroom. I had figured out, in the hours that I'd spent waiting for my opportunity, that her room was the most likely place.

As I opened her bedroom door, I felt a bit like a burglar. It wasn't like I was banned from Mum's room or anything. It was just that I had no reason to go in it if Mum wasn't there. The bed was made with its pink duvet cover lying all smooth and the cushions plumped up and leaning against the headboard. Mum kept it really tidy. Mum's dressing table was under the window, and all her bottles of make-up remover and moisturiser were all neatly lined up in order of size. On the other side was her perfume, her hairbrush and her black, shiny make-up bag. The room smelled of Mum and I breathed her in.

I headed straight for the wardrobe. Time was ticking and I didn't have long. It wasn't far to the shops, and Mum had only gone to pick up a few things for tea. I needed to move quick. I opened the wardrobe door and it creaked really loudly. That made me jump. I don't know why, because that door has always creaked. I must hear it five times a day but it's different when you're sneaking about. Everything makes you jump!

The wardrobe had a rail that was jam-packed with Mum's clothes, and then there was a shelf at the top, and two drawers at the bottom where Mum kept her tights and knickers and stuff. I started with the shelf, dragging the stool over from the dressing table so that I could reach. Because it was Mum's space, it was madly tidy, not a bit like the chaos in my wardrobe. There were neat rows of shoeboxes, and each one had a yellow post-it note label with a description of the shoes inside – brown court, pink flats, that kind of thing. I opened the lids on a couple of them but the labels were all right. There was one other box that looked promising, but when I peeped inside, it just had some old bits of rubbish in it – a china rabbit with a broken ear, a diary with a little padlock from 1985, a cycling proficiency badge. There were no papers, so I put the lid back on and pushed it back into position.

I jumped down but not too heavily so that I wouldn't disturb Mrs Marshall. Then I pushed aside the clothes so I could see if there was anything on the floor of the wardrobe. And there it was, right at the back. The black box file. I slid it out, and sitting on the floor with my legs out in front of me, I placed it carefully on my lap. My heart was beating so hard that I thought Mum would be able to hear it at the shops. With my hands shaking like mad, I pushed the little button on the side and lifted the lid gently. Right on top were our maroon passports and the blue European health cards. I took those out first and put them on the carpet. Then I started to flick through the papers. I wasn't sure what I was looking for, but I assumed that it would say 'Birth Certificate' on it somewhere. There were papers from the bank and something about my child benefit and lots of stuff in brown envelopes. I was starting to feel a bit panicky. Mum could be back at any minute, and if she caught me, I'd have to tell her what I was up to.

I tried to think clearly. My birth certificate was never needed, so it must be at the bottom of the box. Quickly I pulled everything out and worked from the bottom up. The third document was my birth certificate. It was cream with green swirls on it. I held it in my hands, trying to take in what it said. At first it didn't make any sense. The words were jumping about all over the place, and I couldn't seem to focus clearly enough to read them. Then I made myself concentrate, and there it was. Mother – Alison Jane Cooper. Father – Richard Michael Cooper.

I just sat there with the birth certificate in my hands and stared at it. I could have cried. All that effort and sneaking about, and it just told me what I already knew, the names of Mum and Dad. I should have known that it wouldn't be that simple. Otherwise, people would be tracking down their birth parents left, right and centre.

I folded the certificate, making sure that I followed the same

deep creases as before, and slipped it back into the box. I felt
like someone had pulled my plug out. I was certain that finding
my birth mother would be the answer to all my problems, but
I'd run into a brick wall before I'd even got started, and now it
looked like I'd never be able to find her.

I was just putting everything away when a little flash of pink
caught my eye. I pulled whatever it was out of the pile. It was a
card with a picture of a stork holding a smiling baby in a bundle
from its beak. Inside the message read 'Congratulations Ali
and Rick on the arrival of Kitty Rose. Lots of love, Louise.'

I had no idea who Louise was. Whoever she'd been, she must
have floated out of our lives in the last twelve years, because
Mum didn't have any friends called Louise as far as I knew.
There were no other saved cards. I wondered what was so
special about this one. I turned it over in my hands, and there
on the back in Mum's handwriting was the date of my birthday
and a name. Julia Caroline Boniface. Unusual. I'd never even
heard of anyone being called Boniface before.

I looked at it again to make sure that I'd read it right. It didn't
seem to be connected to anything else on the card. The name
was just written on the back in small, neat capitals. Maybe
Louise was a red herring, and what was important about the
card was this writing. And then it hit me why Mum had kept
it for all these years. This must be her. The woman who had
me and gave me away – Julia Caroline Boniface.

I just sat there staring at the words. I couldn't tell you how
they made me feel. I didn't really feel anything at all. It was a
bit like being told about something in a history lesson that had
happened a long time ago and to somebody else. It just didn't
feel real, like it had no connection to me at all. And yet it did.
These words stood for the woman who brought me into the

world. If there had been no Julia Caroline Boniface, then there would have been no Kathryn Rose Cooper.

I don't know how long I sat there staring at the card, but the next thing I knew, I could hear voices downstairs, and I realised that Mum must be home and was talking to Mrs Marshall. Quickly I put the card back in the box and scooped all the other papers, including the passports, back in on top of it. Then I closed the lid, pushed the box into its place at the back of the wardrobe, put the stool away by the dressing table and sneaked back into the lounge. I was just finding a magazine to look at when I heard Mum's key turn in the lock.

'Hi,' she shouted as she came in. 'Can you come and give me a hand with this shopping, please, Kitty Cat?'

And that was it. We went into the kitchen and started cooking tea, and I didn't have a chance to think about it again until I was in bed. It was only then, as I lay in the dark wondering what Julia Caroline Boniface might look like, that I realised that I hadn't put the papers back in the box in the right order. If Mum had any reason to go in that box, then she might notice that I'd been in it too.

Chapter 6

I was dying to tell Lydia what I'd discovered, but she wasn't at school the next day, which was annoying. I texted her and she replied that there wasn't much wrong with her but her mum thought she was at death's door, so she was having a day on the sofa. That would never wash with my mum! There are no sickies chucked around here. Lydia said she'd be back the next day, so I had to keep my enormous news to myself.

Lydia not being at school didn't really make much difference to my day, because of us not being in the same class, but I did see Chloe and Jess Bell looking a bit lost at break time. They seemed to annoy one another but they couldn't leave each other alone. I'd never taken much notice of them until they started to muscle in on Lydia, but it didn't seem like they had many friends of their own. I had plenty of other people to kick around with at break, but I kept sneaking a look at them. Part of me was glad that they looked lonely, which I know isn't that nice but I didn't care. After all, they'd been mean to me.

After school I virtually ran home so that I would have the maximum amount of time on the computer before Mum got back. I raced up the stairs, calling out to Mrs Marshall on my way, opened the door and dumped my bag in the hall before heading straight into the lounge. Our ancient PC was sitting on the little makeshift desk that was really a shelf in the corner. I turned it on. It always took forever to boot up, so I went to make myself a cup of tea whilst I waited. By the time I came back into the lounge, it was ready to go. I opened up Wikipedia and searched for volcanoes so that I had something to open really quickly in case Mum came in, and then I went onto Google. Then I stopped. I wasn't sure what to do next.

I tried typing 'adoption' into the search box. Lots of pages about how to adopt a baby popped up. That was no good. We'd done that bit. No need for an adoption agency. I tried 'how to find your birth mother', and immediately there were hundreds of sites all promising to find Julia Caroline Boniface for me. I clicked on one that said 'Find your birth mother for free', which sounded promising. I certainly hadn't reckoned on having to pay to find her. The webpage was all words typed really close together with flashing adverts down the left-hand side. It was hard to read and understand, but it seemed to be suggesting a number of steps. Step one: find out everything you can about your birth mother. Well, duh! Step two: post details on adoption forums so that you can talk to other people who might know your mother.

There was no way that was an option! It was hard enough searching this without setting up a trail a mile wide for Mum to follow. She wasn't amazing on the computer but she wasn't completely hopeless either. If I started getting messages from a forum, she'd notice straightaway and get suspicious.

I closed that site down and tried another. 'Find your birth mother for £99' it read. Where was I going to get ninety-nine pounds from?

This was going to be harder than I thought. I had assumed that you could just put the name into an adoption site and up she would pop, preferably with a photo, but it seemed it was not as straightforward as that. Or maybe it was? I looked quickly at the clock in the corner of the screen. I probably had about half an hour left before Mum got home from work. I went back to Google and just typed her name into the box – 'Julia Caroline Boniface'. And there she was. Well, I didn't exactly know it was her or whether all these entries were the same person. There was a Facebook page, a Linked-in profile, a 192 search. I didn't have a Facebook account – something else that Mum didn't think was appropriate – so I clicked on the 192 search.

There was only one Julia Caroline Boniface. Thank goodness she wasn't called Smith or something. And there was her address. It was in London with a W1 postcode. It gave her age as being 26–30. Was that right? I quickly did the maths. That would have made her between fourteen and eighteen when she had me.

All at once I had butterflies and goosebumps as I worked out what this meant. She'd given me away not because she didn't love me but because she was too young to look after me properly. Someone had probably made her do it. I reckoned that, given those circumstances, she would be delighted to hear from me.

Quickly I grabbed a square of paper from the memo block that I'd bought Mum for her birthday, and carefully copied out the address. I didn't put her name on it so that if Mum did come across it, she wouldn't think anything of it, and anyway, I was hardly likely to forget her name. It was etched across my mind now. I folded the paper and put it in my skirt pocket and started methodically deleting the history on the computer. I knew that that wouldn't remove my trail completely, but Mum wouldn't know how to check.

Then I went over to the bookshelf and reached down the battered copy of *London A-Z* to find out exactly where her address was. I knew that a W1 postcode meant that it was somewhere posh. I scanned the index for Buchanan Gardens and then realised that if I went onto Google Earth, I would be able to see a picture. It took me ages to get the page loaded, and all the time, I was listening out for Mum coming up the stairs. I urged the computer to work faster. I wasn't sure when I'd get another chance to look without her nosing over my shoulder.

Finally, just as I was about to hit refresh for the hundredth time, up it popped. I just sat and stared. It was one of those really posh houses that you sometimes see on TV dramas, four storeys high with smart black railings outside and an ornate lamp over the front door. The upstairs windows had little stone balconies. I panned the camera round and saw that there was a fenced garden with grass and trees on the other side of the road. It looked like another world from our little flat in Woodston.

Could this really be where my birth mother hung out? So near and yet so far from where I was. I started imagining what she might be like. I'd obviously had these thoughts already over the course of the last few days, but now I had something concrete to hang my imaginings on. I felt like a kid who dreams that they were adopted and that their real family are royalty. Julia Caroline Boniface probably wasn't actual royalty, but she was certainly pretty different to Kitty Cooper.

Chapter 7

The problem with all this sneaking about was that it was making me feel guilty. It had been a while since Mum and I had anything even approaching a row, and so I was starting to wonder whether I'd been a bit hasty with my searching. Perhaps the plan wasn't such a great idea after all. Of course, the person I would normally talk to about this kind of thing was the one person that I couldn't tell – Mum. So I had to go with the second-best option – Lydia.

Lydia was back at school the next day. At break I tried to tell her as cryptically as I could that I had something to talk to her about. After much signalling with my eyes over the tops of people's heads, I finally got it across to her that we needed some time on our own. I thought it might be difficult to sort, what with her little limpets, but she shook the Bell twins off really easily simply by telling them that she was spending her lunchtime with me. They didn't look very pleased, but I felt ten feet tall as Lydia and I walked off together. We decided to do circuits of the tennis courts. We wouldn't be on our own exactly, but unless someone walked along behind us, no one would overhear our conversation.

'I think I've found her,' I said when I was sure that we were far enough away from flapping ears.

'Really? That's fantastic,' said Lydia, her eyes wide and shining as she gripped my arm so tightly I could feel her fingers through my blazer. 'Tell me everything!'

'Well,' I began. 'I found my birth certificate in a box in Mum's wardrobe. It was right at the bottom underneath some papers. But it just had Mum's and Dad's names on it.'

Lydia looked disappointed and was about to say something, but I put my hand up to show her that there was more to come and carried on.

'But … under that was a card with a name written on the back in Mum's writing, and my birthday. Julia Caroline Boniface, that's the name. I think she must be my birth mother. Otherwise, why would Mum have kept it?'

'Are you sure?' asked Lydia, frowning hard.

I could tell from her voice that she thought it all seemed a bit unlikely, and my heart sank. I needed Lydia to be as excited as I was.

'Well, not sure exactly,' I said. 'But I reckon it's a pretty good guess. There was no other reason why Mum would have kept that one card as far as I could tell, and the name is kind of hidden on the back. Plus it's all I've got to go on,' I added.

Lydia didn't speak for a moment as she thought through what I'd just said.

'Kitty Boniface?' she said then. 'It's not as nice as Kitty Cooper.'

I felt so relieved. Lydia was agreeing with me that this must be my birth mother. It wasn't just my crackpot idea.

'Well, that doesn't matter, because I'm not going to change my name just because I've found my birth mother. It's good that it's so weird, though, because otherwise I might never have found her.'

I told her about the adoption sites and how you needed to pay to trace people. Lydia listened carefully, eyes widening when I told her how much the online searches were.

'But then,' I said, 'I just put her name into Google, and there she was with her address and everything. And get this!'

I paused for dramatic effect.

'She lives in Mayfair. A place called Buchanan Gardens. I looked on Google Earth. It's well posh. She must be loaded to have a house there.'

I thought for a split second that I saw disappointment flicker across Lydia's face. Perhaps she hoped that my birth mother would be nothing special or that I wouldn't be able to find her at all. But then the look disappeared as quickly as it had arrived, and I had the excited Lydia back.

'So what are you going to do next?'

Lydia sounded almost as excited as I was. I paused before I spoke. The truth was that I still had no idea what I was going to do.

'I don't know,' I confessed. 'It feels kind of wrong going to track her down, like I'm being disloyal to Mum or something.'

'But you're not being. It's not like you're trying to push your Mum out of the picture. You're just trying to find someone who can help her. I bet she'll be glad when she finds out. She'll be really grateful to have another person on hand to help.'

Lydia had a knack of always saying the right thing. It was one of the reasons why she was my best friend. But I still needed a bit more reassurance.

'Do you really think so?' I asked. 'I was starting to think that it wasn't such a great plan after all.'

'Yes!' she said, nodding her head frantically at me.

She stopped dead in her tracks. I stopped too. Then she

turned to face me and looked straight into my eyes to make sure that I was really listening to her.

'This is a great plan,' she said. 'The best. And you should definitely get in touch with her. If you don't, you're going to spend the rest of your life wondering. Even if she turns out to be a nightmare, I think you need to know, don't you?'

I didn't say anything straightaway. I wondered if she was right. Could I come this far and not taken the final few steps? Of course, I already knew the answer. There was absolutely no chance that I could file this information away somewhere and not do anything to track Julia down.

'You're right,' I said, suddenly feeling loads more confident. I knew she was right. I had never felt more sure about anything in my entire life.

'I'm just not totally sure how to do it,' I added.

This was true. I had her name and her address, but what would be the best thing to do next?

'You could just turn up,' Lydia suggested.

Even though I had no plan, I knew that that was the wrong way to go. I shook my head.

'I can't do that! What if it isn't her? What if she's got lots of other children and doesn't want to know me? What if she has a heart attack right there on the doorstep?'

'Well, what then? Ring her?'

I shook my head. Just the thought of ringing her up and saying what I had to say made me feel sick.

'I thought I could write to her,' I said. 'Then if she wants to get in touch, she can write back, and if she doesn't or if it isn't her, she can just ignore me.'

'OK,' said Lydia as she mulled the plan over. 'Sounds sensible. What will you say in the letter?'

'I suppose I'll just tell her who I am and ask if she wants to meet me. Then, when I've got to know her a bit, I can see if she wants to help Mum, with the bringing-me-up stuff.'

And then it all seemed really simple.

'I'll do it tonight when Mum thinks I'm doing my homework, and I can post it on the way to school tomorrow. Then I'll just have to wait and see what happens.'

As we began our third circuit of the tennis court, the bell went for the end of lunch. We were just about to turn round and head back to our classrooms, when Lydia stopped and grabbed me. She gave me an enormous hug, and then she said, 'You're doing the right thing, you know, and I'm with you every step of the way.'

I squeezed her back and I knew that she really meant it.

Chapter 8

So that night after school I wrote the letter. I wondered about using the thick, creamy paper that Mum keeps for important letters, but I couldn't get that from the drawer in the lounge without her asking me what I wanted it for. So instead, I dug out some notepaper that Mrs Marshall had bought me for Christmas. Because it was a gift from Mrs Marshall, it had cats on it. Not cute cartoon cats, but pictures of real cats doing catty things like lying in the sun or walking on a fence. I chose one where the cat was looking longingly as a goldfish. I wasn't sure it was perfect, but at least it made me smile. I hoped Julia would like it too.

I wrote out what I wanted to say on a piece of scrap paper first.

Dear Ms Boniface, (I didn't know if she was married or what, so I used 'Ms' just to be on the safe side.)

You don't know me but I think I might be your birth daughter. (Direct and to the point. No messing.) *I was wondering whether you wanted to meet me, as there's something really important that I want*(then I crossed 'want' out and wrote 'need' instead) *to talk to you about.*

My mobile number is - . Please ring or text me to say whether I

am your daughter and whether you want to meet up.
    Yours sincerely,
    Kitty Rose Cooper.

I read the letter through several times, and then, when I'd decided that there wasn't anything else I needed to say, I wrote it out really neatly on the cat notepaper. Then I copied the Buchanan Gardens address from the slip of paper onto the envelope. I had no stamp. I could have taken one from Mum's purse without asking and she would never have known, but that felt wrong, so I decided to buy one on my way to school. I put the letter inside my maths textbook, where I was pretty sure Mum wouldn't find it, and put the book in my school bag ready for the next day.

The following morning, I toyed with the idea in my head one last time, but I still hadn't changed my mind, so I called in at the minimart and bought a stamp. I stuck it onto the top corner neatly. Then I kissed the envelope for good luck and popped it in the postbox on the corner of Church Street. And that was that. The deed was done.

I didn't know how long it might take for something to happen. I'd bought a first-class stamp, so I reckoned that, as the letter was only crossing London, it should arrive the following day. My birth mother, Julia, would likely be at work during the day, so she wouldn't get it until she got home, and then she might want to think about it for a bit. I calculated that I was unlikely to hear anything for at least a couple of days. That seemed a long way off, so I relaxed a little bit. I can't say that I forgot about it, because it was always there at the back of my mind, but I managed to get on with things without worrying.

51

Anyway, I had other things to worry about. Kyle Johnson, the coolest boy in the year, was about to turn thirteen, and he was having a party at his house. He was so cool, partly because he was pretty good-looking in a 'boy band' kind of way, and partly because he had this big brother who everyone seemed to idolise. I didn't like him though. He was one of those people who look over your shoulder when they are talking to you in case there's someone more interesting in the room. Not that he ever talked to me. I was way too far down the food chain for him to be bothered with.

Anyway, we all knew Kyle's party was coming up, because he'd been going on about it for weeks. His parents were going out, or so he said, and his brother Louis was in charge. Louis was seventeen and had left school at the end of the year before to go to college. Kyle said that he had done the world's best playlist, which was going to blast out from some immense sound system that he'd rigged up, and that his brother was going to get some alcohol. I wasn't sure I entirely believed this. Kyle talked a lot, but not much of what he said ever seemed to come true. Also, Louis was only seventeen, so I wasn't sure where he was going to get drinks from. I discussed my doubts with Lydia, and she agreed that even if Louis had beer, he was hardly going to share it with any of Kyle's mates. We concluded that Kyle was all talk, which we knew anyway. Not that this made any difference, as there was absolutely no chance of me being invited to his party.

As soon as I got to school, I could tell that something was going on. The place was buzzing. I picked up, from overhearing a conversation by the lockers, that Kyle had set up an event on Facebook. It wasn't a general thing. He had invited the people that you'd expect – the popular boys and all the pretty girls. As Mum wouldn't let me have a Facebook account, I knew I wouldn't have been on the list, but then I would never have been invited even if I had had Facebook. I wasn't part of the cool-kids crowd. I was way too dull for that!

Kyle was in my form though, and when I got to the classroom, he was already in there sitting at his desk on the second row, next to the window. He was swinging back on his chair so the front legs lifted off the ground and looking as if he owned the place. How funny it would be, I thought, if he fell. As usual, he had his gang gathered round him, and he was going through a list of the people he'd invited. My desk is at the front on the opposite side of the room, so I just sat down and tried to look busy sorting out my books for first period. Kyle was talking in a really loud voice so that everyone would know about his precious party, but then our form teacher came in, told Kyle off for swinging on his chair and took the register, and so that was the last I heard of the party until break.

I was with Lydia by the shelter, and the Bell twins were hanging around pointlessly as usual. They were being all giddy and stupid because they'd been invited to the party. They were the kind of girls that always get invited to boys' parties – you know the sort. Lydia hadn't got an invite either but she didn't seem that bothered. She mouthed silently at me to ask whether I'd posted the letter. I nodded but the Bells didn't notice, because just then, Kyle and a couple of his mates came up to talk to Jess.

'Did you get my message?' he asked her, but you could tell that he knew she had and was just asking so we'd wonder what they were talking about.

'Yes, thanks. Chlo and me'll be there. Seven at your house, right?'

'Yup. Seven till late. It's going to be a bangin' night. You should bring your mate.'

He looked straight at Lydia, who was standing there looking gorgeous with her long legs and her blonde hair and her pretty smile. I prayed that she wouldn't go all giggly and stupid, and of course she didn't. She just looked him up and down, and said, 'Yeah. Maybe. Can Kitty come?'

This put Kyle on the spot. He obviously didn't want me there, but he couldn't really say no to Lydia, so he just sort of grunted a yes. He didn't look at me at all.

'Great,' Lydia said. 'Well, I might see you then.'

She just dismissed him. I love Lydia. She's so good at that kind of thing. Kyle didn't know quite how to react. He was used to calling the shots. So he turned to Chloe and Jess, put an arm round each waist and led them off towards the tennis courts, leaving me and Lydia on our own. As they walked, Jess threw her head back to laugh at something he'd said and flicked her hair around. Me and Lydia just looked at one another and burst into giggles.

'So will you go?' I asked her.

She cocked her head on one side and wrinkled her nose.

'I don't know,' she said slowly. 'Maybe. I mean, Kyle's an idiot but it might be a laugh. What about you?'

'Well, if you're going …' I said. 'I wouldn't fancy it on my own. I'll need to ask Mum, but if I tell her I'm not that bothered about it, then she might let me. It's not for a couple weeks yet, is it? I'll have to see what happens between now and then.'

'You might have a new mum by then,' Lydia said, but I corrected her.

'It's not that I'm getting a new mum. It's more like getting a reserve one. Like in a football team. A substitute mum in case the first one gets injured or something. Anyway, she's got to get in touch first. It might not be her, and if it is her, she might not want anything to do with me. She did get rid of me after all.'

I needed to act like I wasn't that excited, even with Lydia, in case the whole thing went wrong, but actually, I was starting to feel pretty positive about it all. Now that I'd discovered that Julia Caroline Boniface was only a teenager when she gave me away, it seemed to make more sense. She felt more human somehow, kinder and more approachable.

I didn't want to tell Lydia all this though. It was best if these thoughts stayed in my head for now. Just in case.

Chapter 9

I was in the bath when I got the text. I always take my phone with me when I have a bath, but I put it on the floor by the door so that it doesn't accidentally fall in. Even though my phone then was nothing flash, I knew that it was the only one that I was likely to get, so I looked after it. I'd run the bath nice and deep, and put one of the strawberry bath bombs in it. I'd been saving it since Christmas but it was a bit of a disappointment, if I'm honest. It didn't explode or anything like a bomb should. It just fizzed a bit and then sank to the bottom and dissolved. There weren't even any bubbles. It just made the water go kind of milky, but it did smell really nice, like strawberry milkshake.

I'd tied my hair up in a messy bun and I had a copy of *Heat* that Lydia had passed on to me. I felt quite grown up really. I'd just settled down in the water, carefully making sure that I didn't get the magazine wet, when the text came in. I don't swear but I said something equivalent. I didn't move. It was too much effort to stand up and get out of the bath to retrieve the phone. It would probably just be Lydia telling me something about some rubbish she was watching on the telly or a bit of online gossip, so I just ignored it and settled back down to enjoy my bath. It must have been about five minutes later when it suddenly crossed my mind that it might be from Julia.

I stood up really quickly then. All the water swooshed to one end of the bath and then swooshed back to the other. I thought it was going to flood out and make a horrible mess all over the floor. I held my breath and just watched it, but gradually the water fell back down to where it belonged without a drop escaping. Phew! I hopped out onto the bath mat and grabbed my towel from the radiator to dry my hand before picking up the phone.

Then I stopped dead. I just stood there, stark naked, dripping on the bath mat with my legs all pink from the hot water. I couldn't breathe. My heart was beating hard in my chest. I told myself to calm down. It might not be from her at all. In fact, it would probably be Lydia. But what if it was her? What if she didn't want anything to do with me? Did I want to know that? Was I ready for that?

Well, I didn't really have any choice. I would have to look eventually. I wrapped myself up in the towel, picked up the phone and sat with my back against the door. I looked down at the screen. It was a number that the phone didn't recognise. Not Lydia, then. Not anyone I knew. A wrong number maybe?

I clicked on 'Open Message' and there it was. A message from my birth mother. At first my head was spinning so fast that I couldn't actually read what it said. Then slowly the words began to fall into some kind of order and I read.

Hi Kitty. What a surprise to get your letter. Would love to meet up. Text me and tell me when you can come. Juju xxx

And that was it. I read it four or five times and then I climbed back into the bath to have a think. It all seemed very straightforward. She was glad to hear from me and she wanted to meet up. Simple.

'Juju'? I puzzled over that for a while until I realised that it was short for Julia. Three kisses too – the perfect number. Not just one that looks like you don't mean it, but not too many, which always looks massively over the top. As I lay there with the water cooling around me, I decided that this was the best response that I could have hoped for. Nice and positive but also friendly and encouraging. All my fears just floated away in the cooling strawberry-milkshake water.

So now all I had to do was to find a way to get there. It was about twenty minutes by train into St Pancras, and then I could catch the Tube down to Mayfair. If I spent an hour with Julia – Juju – then I would need to be gone for about three hours altogether. That wouldn't be too difficult. I could tell Mum that I was at Lydia's, and then Lydia could cover for me. The plan was all coming together, but the bath water was getting really chilly, so I climbed out and got dried.

'Kitty. It's nearly bedtime. Are you out of that bath yet?'

Mum always kept a close eye on the time in the evenings. No sneakily staying up for me. I shouted back that I was just getting dried and I wouldn't be long. Then I sat back down against the door and set about typing a reply.

Hi. I can come on Saturday afternoon around 3. Is that OK? Shall I come to your house? Kitty xxx

Simple and clear. I hit send. Within moments the reply was there.

That's great. Mine is the top doorbell. Can't wait to meet you. Juju xxx

Before I left the bathroom, I saved the phone number to my contacts. I pondered over what to write to start with, but then I just put 'Juju'. After all, that was my birth mother's name!

After Mum had come in to say goodnight, I lay awake in the dark for a long time, just wondering. I tried to picture what my birth mum would look like. All I knew was that she was younger than Mum, lived in Mayfair and called herself Juju xxx. Even though I tried not to, it was really hard not to imagine her as being glamorous and rich. After all, the three facts that I had so far could easily point in that direction.

Then, just as I was dropping off to sleep, I was battered by a heart-stopping pang of guilt. I had taken this enormous step and I hadn't even told Mum. I told Mum almost everything. I always had done. This was my first proper secret from her – first of many, as it turned out – but then again, as I was doing this to make Mum's life easier, it would hardly be fair if she got cross with me. Anyway, it was still early days. If Juju (it still sounded strange to me, that name) wasn't interested in me, then I need never tell Mum that I'd found her, and I could forget all about it. I couldn't help wondering, though, if Juju was now in my life for keeps.

Chapter 10

I hadn't told Mum about Juju, but obviously, I had to tell Lydia. I texted her and asked her to meet me early at the corner of Church Street so that we get good talking time in on the way to school, especially if we walked slowly. It was a lovely day, clear, bright and full of promise. I got there first, so I sat on the wall and waited for Lydia.

The street was full of people zipping backwards and forwards, all getting on with their own stuff. I wondered if any of them were related to me. I might have cousins and whatnot all over the place. Would I recognise them if I saw them? I struggled to imagine what it would be like to share features with someone else. 'Ooh, she has her mum's nose' or 'her dad's eyes.' That kind of stuff. Lydia looked just like her brother Callum. Mum said it must be strong genes in the Tench family. My genes were still a mystery.

I was just contemplating this when Lydia arrived. We set off walking to school at a snail's pace.

'So, what's the big news?' Lydia asked.

I could hear a little bit of sarcasm in her voice, which I didn't like much – too much time spent with those Bell twins. I ignored it. She would be interested enough when I told her what had happened.

'I texted my mum last night, I mean, my birth mother.'

I waited. I wanted a proper reaction, having been unimpressed with her opening comment. I got one.

'Oh my God!' she squealed so loudly that a woman, who was walking by with a little Yorkshire terrier on a lead, turned round to stare at her and then tutted loudly.

'What did you say? Did she text back? Are you going to see her? When?'

This was more like it. I smiled, enjoying the moment. Lydia tugged on my sleeve to get me to talk.

'Well,' I said slowly. 'She texted me first. She got my letter and she said she was glad to hear from me and wanted to meet up. Wait. Look.'

I pulled my phone out of my blazer pocket and flicked through until I got to Juju's message. I offered it to Lydia and she took the phone from me and peered at the screen.

'Juju? That's a bit random but I like it. It's unusual and 'Julia' sounds a bit stuck-up. So? What did you text back?'

'Have a look,' I said, and so she scrolled down and read all three messages.

'That's amazing. All sorted just like that.'

'Yup! Just like that.'

I was enjoying this. It wasn't often that I had something exciting to talk about, seeing as Mum never let me go anywhere to do anything exciting.

'So what are you going to do?' Lydia asked.

I could see the possibilities and potential pitfalls were all racing through her mind. You could almost see the cogs going round in her brain from the thoughtful expression on her face.

'I assume you're planning on going?' she asked.

'Of course,' I said, nodding furiously. 'Will you cover for me?

I thought maybe I could tell Mum that I was coming over to yours for a bit on Saturday afternoon and that we were going to the precinct.'

Lydia thought this through as we walked along, tapping her mouth with her finger.

'Yes,' she said after a moment. 'That could work. I was already planning to meet Chloe and Jess down there, so it isn't really a lie.'

I noted that she had made a plan that didn't involve me again. She saw that I'd realised, and blushed just a little bit, but I decided to ignore it. This was too important to get bogged down with minor trivialities like the Bell twins.

'Well, that will work really well, then, because if my Mum does ring your house for some reason, your Mum will just say that you're out at the precinct, and you can tell her that you're meeting me there.'

I could feel myself getting carried away with the intrigue of it all. It was quite good fun, this sneaking about. I felt like a spy.

'And then,' I continued, 'I can catch a train down into town and make my way to her house.'

Then out of nowhere, the enormity of what I was doing hit me again. Lies! Intrigue! Finding random parents! I'd never done anything like this before. I stopped walking and put my hand on Lydia's arm. I felt a bit sick.

'What if she hates me? What if I get there and she won't let me in or there's no one there?'

'Then you'll turn round and come straight back home,' said Lydia, putting her arm around my shoulder and giving me a little squeeze. 'But why would she hate you? You're lovely. And it's obvious that she wants to get in touch because if she didn't, she wouldn't have texted you. It'll be fine. Don't worry. Do you want me to come with you?'

Lydia coming too was a new idea and it felt really appealing. If I took her with me, then we could have a laugh on the train and find the place together. Then, if it turned out that Juju was actually a witch in disguise, we could run away. Together. But even as I thought all this, I knew that this was something that I had to do alone.

'I would love you to come with me,' I said, squeezing her arm as we walked, 'but I think I'd better go on my own. It'll be hard enough for Juju with one long-lost daughter turning up on her doorstep without her dragging along her mate too. Maybe next time though?'

Lydia nodded her head. She could see that I was right.

'So,' she said, 'do you know where you're going?'

'Not exactly,' I admitted. 'I've got the address, so I'll just have to work it out before I go, and hope for the best. Buchanan Gardens looks like quite a big square on Google Earth. I'm sure it won't be that difficult to find.'

We weren't far from school now, and I could hear the murmur of voices growing louder. Lydia took a step so that she was standing in front of me, blocking my way, and then she looked right into my eyes as if she were searching for something there.

'You are really OK with this, aren't you?' she asked me, and she looked so serious that at first I wanted to giggle. We'd been through a lot together, Lydia and me, and she knew me better than anyone in the whole world. Except Mum, of course.

I sucked my lips in around my teeth and then nodded, not quite trusting my words to come out evenly.

'Because you don't have to do it if you don't want to,' she

continued. 'No one knows but us and I'm not going to tell anyone.'

Despite everything that had happened recently with the Bell twins, I believed her. She was my best friend and I knew she could keep a secret.

'You can just walk away and we'll forget all about it. I'm sure we can come up with some other cunning plan to make your mum see sense and let you get past toddlerhood.'

This made me smile and I gave her a huge hug.

'No,' I said. 'I'm totally one hundred per cent sure. I need to meet her this first time, and if it doesn't work out, then that's fine. I just won't see her again. But now I've come this far, I couldn't go back, even if I wanted to.'

'Well, if you're sure …' Lydia said.

We were just outside the gates now, and the bell rang loud and shrill to announce our arrival.

'And I need a word with you, young lady,' I said in my sternest teacher voice.

'Now what?' Lydia asked.

She was biting her lip and looked genuinely worried. I enjoyed the moment.

'What are you thinking, planning to go off on a Saturday afternoon with those Bell twins and not taking me?'

I tried really hard to hold on to the angry face that I was pulling, but I just couldn't do it, and I started to giggle.

'Well,' she said, shrugging her shoulders at me. 'What's a girl supposed to do when her best mate goes up to the West End to hobnob with the smart set without her?'

We were still laughing as we walked through the school gates. I was sure that with Lydia at my side, nothing would go wrong. But that state of affairs didn't last that long.

Chapter 11

When I woke up on Saturday morning, I had that weird feeling you get when you know it's a special day but you can't remember why. I lay in bed looking up at my ceiling. There's a dark patch in the corner where the roof leaked. It sometimes looks like an upside-down elephant, but it was too light outside, and the shape just looked like a slightly darker patch of plaster.

So today was the day. I examined my mood carefully, but I was definitely more excited about what was to come than nervous. I had my route worked out, money for the train, and my outfit planned. I was totally ready to meet Juju.

Then Mum threw a spanner in the works.

We were having breakfast, which for me is always Shreddies and then toast with strawberry jam. I could have something different if I want, but I never want. Anyway, I was eating my cereal, and Mum was pottering about putting things away.

'I thought we might go shopping this afternoon,' she said as she stacked the pasta pan carefully on top of all the others. 'It'll be your birthday soon, and I thought you might want some new clothes to match your new sophisticated teenage image.'

Mum turned to look me, raised her eyebrows and then winked. This was obviously her way of making up for not letting me do as much as Lydia and the others. I suppose she wanted me to know that she did understand that I was growing up. And normally, it would have been perfect. I love shopping for clothes with Mum. It's great! We start off with a fixed budget in mind, but then she always gets carried away and ends up spending more because she can't resist treating me. Then we have a McDonald's on the way home, and I do a little fashion show for her of all the things that we've bought. We don't do it very often, but when we do, it is absolutely my favourite thing.

But not today …

Mum must have sensed my reluctance. It wouldn't have been hard. Normally, when she suggests one of these shopping trips, you don't see me for dust as I race to get ready to leave.

'What's the matter?' she asked. 'Don't you fancy it?'

I looked at her and I could see the disappointment in her face. She must have enjoyed our trips as much as I did. Her shoulders sagged and it made my heart hurt. I didn't know how I would bear it.

'It's not that,' I said quickly. 'It's a great idea and I'd love to go, but do we have to do it today? Couldn't we go tomorrow instead?'

I smiled my widest smile at her to show that I did still really want to go.

'Why? What's on today?' she asked, but I could tell by her voice that the magic moment was gone.

'Oh, not much. It's just that I'd arranged to go to the precinct with Lydia.'

As I made my excuse, I could hear how lame it sounded. I was turning down a trip to go to the big shops with my mum and her credit card in favour of a wander around the little local precinct with Lydia, who I saw every day.

'Oh,' said Mum in that really disappointed voice that she uses when I have done something that she doesn't approve of. 'Well, couldn't you rearrange that? I mean, that is something you could do any day, isn't it? It doesn't have to be today.'

What was I do to? I could see my plan disappearing before my very eyes. If I went with Mum, I would have to text Juju to cancel her, and who could say whether she'd be happy to rearrange for another day? She might change her mind, and then my chance would be lost. And if I went shopping with Mum, it would be difficult to then sneak off 'shopping with Lydia' for three hours that afternoon, even if we were back in time for me to go at all.

As Mum stared at me, waiting for me to speak, I tried desperately to think of a solution, but my brain felt like cotton wool, and no ideas came. I knew how hurt and let down Mum was going to be but I had to meet Juju. I had no choice, not when I'd come this far.

'Couldn't we go tomorrow?' I tried again, but I could see that it was no use.

'No,' she said in that snappish way that she has. 'I can't do tomorrow. I've got too much else to do. It doesn't matter, Kitty. I thought it might be fun but we can always do it some other time.'

Then she turned her back on me and started running the water to do the washing-up.

I felt terrible. If only I'd known what she was planning, I could have worked around it, but my plan was made and I couldn't unmake it.

'I'm sorry, Mum. I really am,' I said, but she wasn't really listening any more.

I did the drying-up without saying much. We hadn't had

a row or anything, but there was an atmosphere between us that hadn't been there before. I didn't like it but I couldn't do anything to make it go away. I knew that even if I changed my mind and cancelled Juju, the trip with Mum would be spoiled anyway.

Then I realised with a horrible sinking feeling that Mum hadn't actually said I could go to the precinct with Lydia. If she said no to that, then I had wrecked the whole mother–daughter shopping trip for nothing. I knew that I had to tread really carefully now. I put the last plate away in the cupboard, and then I asked in a voice so quiet that I might have been a mouse in disguise, 'So, is it OK if I meet Lydia in the precinct this afternoon?'

Mum didn't even look at me as she headed for the kitchen door.

'Yep,' she said sharply without turning round. 'Whatever.'

And then she left.

I felt so bad. I can't tell you. In trying not to let Juju down, I had badly hurt Mum's feelings. Now she would think I preferred to spend my time with Lydia than with her, which wasn't true, and that I would rather buy my clothes without her there, which wasn't true either. I loved our girly shopping trips. I almost shouted after her to say that I'd changed my mind and would love to go with her, but what would be the point? I would lose Juju, and the shopping trip was wrecked anyway because I hadn't jumped at it when she first mentioned it. I felt like crying but I didn't, because then Mum would want to know what was wrong, and I didn't really trust myself not to let the whole thing come rushing out. So I just stood there feeling rubbish.

The gloss was kind of gone from the day then, and even

though I tried to be excited, like I had been when I'd first woken up, I couldn't get the picture of Mum's disappointed face out of my mind. When it was time to head for the station, I still felt incredibly guilty. I needed to catch the 14.12 out of Woodston to get there in time. I'd got dressed carefully in my denim shorts with my Converses and little grey top with the Peter Pan collar that Mum said always brought out the colour of my eyes. My hair was down, and I had my black satchel with my purse and my phone and the directions to Buchanan Gardens, which I had painstakingly worked out from the A-Z. I was ready. I took a couple of deep breaths and then I went out into the corridor and shouted to Mum.

'Right, Mum. I'm off. I'll see you later. Back around five thirty, I think.'

I was just going to head out when Mum came out of the lounge to see me off. She smiled at me but I could tell she was still a bit upset about what had happened. When she spoke, her voice was kind but sad.

'OK, Kitten. Have a lovely time. Remember to be careful, and if the plans change, let me know before you do anything.'

Then she came to me and gave me a big hug. She smelled of washing powder and her perfume and her own special Mum smell. I knew then that everything was going to be OK and that someday we would laugh about this morning. I hugged her back and left the flat. It was starting.

Outside, the day was sunny and warm. The boys from over the road were playing football in the street, racing after the blue-and-white ball to catch it every time a car came too close. I saw Mrs Marshall sitting in her front window with Merlin and a cup of tea, and I waved at her as I walked past, but I didn't slow down. I was focused and I needed to get that train no matter what, so I headed down the street, and with every step I took away from the flat, I felt less guilty and confused.

At the train station, I bought my ticket and waited. The platform was busy with lots of people going to town for Saturday afternoon, and when the train pulled in, I wheedled my way to the front so that I would get a seat.

I ended up sitting next to a lad who must have been about eighteen. He had his pointed black boots on the seat opposite him as if no one had ever told him that you shouldn't put your feet on the seats. In fact, there was a huge sign just there that told you not to do it, but he didn't care. He was that kind of guy. He had his headphones in, but the music was so loud that I could hear it leaking out of his ears and into mine. I didn't recognise the song though. Lots of thrashy guitars and a miserable-sounding voice. He was quite good-looking in a relaxed kind of way, and I tried to peer sideways at the bits of him that I could see from where I was sitting without him noticing. He wouldn't have noticed, of course. I doubt he even realised that a nearly thirteen-year-old girl had sat down next to him. It must be nice to be like him and not care what's going on around you.

As the train got closer to St Pancras, I began to feel a bit nervous. I'd been to town loads of times with Mum but I'd never been on my own before. I was hoping that I could find my way from the train station to the Tube. I knew that I had to catch the Victoria line down to Green Park. I wondered whether people were looking at me and wondering where I was going all on my own, but of course, no one did. Finally, the train pulled into St Pancras, and I joined the scrum at the doors to get off. I saw a sign with an arrow pointing to the Underground straightaway, so I didn't have to be worried, and

I just got pushed along in the crowd until I was standing on the platform. The sign said that the next Tube would be along in two minutes, so I stood reading the adverts for shows and English language schools.

Out of the corner of my eye, I noticed something moving down among the tracks. I thought it was just a leaf to start with, but when I looked more carefully, I saw that it was a little mouse. Its fur was almost completely black, from the dirt, I assumed, and it scampered about over and under the tracks, searching for bits of food that people had dropped. I could feel the breeze that told you the train was coming, and as it got stronger and the noise louder, I got a bit worried about the mouse. It wasn't bothered. It just carried on as if having a gigantic train arrive right in the middle of your house was the most natural thing in the world, which I supposed it was to the mouse. Anyway, I couldn't see where it went, because then the train had arrived, and everyone was pushing to get on whilst all the people who were already on were pushing to get off.

There was nowhere to sit on the Tube, so I squeezed myself into a corner by the doors and held on tight as we made our way down the tracks to Juju. I counted off the stations as they raced by. When we reached Green Park, I got off and headed up to the light of the sunny day. I knew that Buchanan Street was just off Piccadilly, and that would lead me to Buchanan Gardens. I'd even managed, more by luck than judgment, to emerge at the right exit from the Tube. As I headed down Buchanan Street, I had a good feeling about my trip. So far it had run like clockwork. All I had to do now was find the house and ring the top doorbell.

Soon I found the turning for Buchanan Gardens, just like I'd planned, and I took it. The square was even more magnificent than it had looked on Google Earth. The buildings were tall and very clean-looking, and there were boxes at all the windows filled with red geraniums and ivy. Some of the doors had shiny brass signs outside them. I thought these must be the names of the families living inside until I realised that they were offices. I should have realised that it might not be all houses. After all, neither was Fieldview Road. There was the minimart and a dentist and the bookie's just near our front door.

I started looking for number forty-eight. It wasn't difficult, because I could recognise the building from the pictures that I'd seen. And then suddenly there it was. Juju's door had a shiny brass sign too, which just said '48' in black numbers. There were six steps leading up to the front door but no doorbells. My heart started to race. What if I couldn't find it? What if I was in completely the wrong place? I took a deep breath to steady my nerves and then looked around to make sure that I hadn't missed them. I wondered if I should just ring Juju and tell her that I was outside. I was just about to dig in my bag for my phone when I saw through the glass panes in the door that the doorbells were just inside. Carefully I opened the huge black door and stepped in. There to my left were five doorbells. The one at the top had a printed card next to it that said 'Ms J Boniface'.

There she was. I'd found her!

I felt a bit sick, but now was not the time to get cold feet. I pushed the bell and waited. Nothing. I could feel my hands getting clammy as I stood there. I was about to push it again when a voice spoke through the intercom.

'Yes?'

'It's Kitty Cooper. I've come to see Juju, Ms Boniface.'

My voice was all high-pitched and babyish. It didn't sound a bit like me, even to me. The voice on the other end immediately became more welcoming.

'Oh, darling! You made it. Fabulous. Come on up. There's a lift to your right. It's the penthouse.'

And that was it. A click signalled that she had switched the intercom off, and I was left standing there feeling bewildered and excited all at the same time. The door behind me opened and I walked through to the lift. I pressed the call button and waited, shaking slightly, whilst it came to take me to meet my birth mother.

Chapter 12

The lift arrived and I stepped in. It was the poshest lift I'd ever been in. The walls were covered in mirrors. I was reflected back and forth so many times that I almost couldn't tell which was the real me. I twisted myself round to try to see what I looked like from the back, but I kept twisting the wrong way and so I gave up. The lift buttons were brass and so shiny that I could see my face in them as well. I pushed the top one and waited as the door closed and the lift made the short journey to the penthouse.

I'd never been in a penthouse before. I knew from films that the penthouse was the best flat, the one at the top with the best views. I didn't think the views from Juju's flat would be that spectacular. It was hardly a skyscraper, but it still gave me a kick to know that my birth mother lived in the best one. My hands wouldn't stop shaking. I was properly nervous now. I tried to remind myself how friendly her text had been and how nice her voice had sounded just now on the intercom, but it still felt like I had pigeons flying round inside my stomach.

The lift reached the top, stopped, and the doors opened to reveal a cream hallway. There was a tall, thin window out to the street, with a heavy cream-coloured curtain hanging to one side. It was pulled back by a huge gold tassel, and it dangled down and trailed on the carpet. It was far too long, but somehow it looked as if it was supposed to be.

I stepped out into the corridor. It was very quiet and there was no sign of Juju. I was a bit disappointed that she hadn't come out to meet me, but I tried to ignore it. I went to knock on what I assumed was her front door, but as I touched it, it swung open onto a long hallway. There were black-and-white photos in thin black frames hanging on the walls on either side. I wasn't sure what to do, so I shouted out, but when the sound came out of my mouth, it was less of a shout and more a kind of whisper.

'Hello? Is anyone there? It's Kitty. I've come to visit Juju.'

'Come in, darling, come in. I'm in the drawing room. Just come straight down the corridor and it's the room at the end.'

I walked down to where the voice was coming from, passing several closed doors, and then into the 'drawing room', which was really a lounge. The sun was shining through the huge windows, so it was really bright compared to the dark lift and corridor. My eyes struggled to adjust and I blinked a bit whilst I got my bearings.

It was a huge room, all painted in cream. There were three large sofas piled high with cushions in cream and gold, and one of those sofas with only one arm, like the Romans used to have. Hanging from the ceiling was a crystal chandelier that was sending tiny little rainbows dancing all over the walls as the sunlight hit it. The floor was wooden, but not just floorboards like at Lydia's. It was made up of hundreds of little rectangles like tiny toffee-coloured bricks. On top of it in the middle was a really thick cream rug, the sort where your footprint stays in it like snow. It was the most beautiful room I had ever seen.

And there, sitting on one of the sofas with a glossy magazine in her hands, was Juju. The first thing I noticed about her was her hair. It was beautiful thick and blonde hair and cut to just below her shoulders. I remember thinking even then that if she was my mother, how come my hair was 'mousy'? It was straight like mine though. She was wearing a short cream skirt and a white silk blouse. At the end of her very long legs, which were crossed at the ankle, was a pair of spike-heeled gold shoes. It wasn't that tacky gold that you see women at the precinct wearing, but proper classy-looking.

She looked like she was in camouflage against that cream room, but of course, you'd never fail to spot her, because she was so beautiful. Her face was smooth, not a wrinkle in sight, and her skin had a sort of golden glow to it as if she'd just been on holiday. Her make-up was totally perfect. She even had lipstick on, in the house! And when I looked into her eyes, I saw my grey eyes looking back. That was pretty weird, to look at someone who looked like you. Of course, I didn't really look like her – she was glamorous and looked like a movie star – but there was something about her eyes that convinced me straightaway that I had the right woman. She was definitely something to do with me.

She put down her magazine and uncurled her legs. The way she moved reminded me of a cat. She stood up and held her arms out as if she wanted to hug me. I wasn't sure what to do, so I didn't do anything. She put her arms down again.

'Come here, Kitty darling. Let me have a look at you. Kitty is such a pretty name.'

'It's short for Kathryn,' I said, because I didn't know what else to say.

I suddenly felt overwhelmingly shy. My feet seemed to be stuck to the floor. I couldn't move. I just stood where I was and stared at her. I didn't mean to. I know it's rude to stare but I just couldn't help it. In the end she walked over to me. She put her hands on my shoulders and I noticed her nails for the first time. They were very long and the palest pink with white tips, but they didn't look cheap like the girls who wear acrylics at school. They looked like they should be in a magazine advertising hand cream, or diamonds. She bent down so that she was looking straight into my eyes, her eyes, and for a moment I thought she was going to cry, which would have been a bit awkward, but then she recovered herself.

'Come and sit down over here next to me and tell me all about yourself,' she said, and steered me gently by the shoulder until we were both sitting side by side on the sofa she had just left.

'What do you want to know?' I asked. I had no idea what to tell her. 'My name is Kitty Rose Cooper. I'm twelve years old, thirteen next month.'

Then I stopped and blushed a bit. Of course, she knew that. She had given birth to me. I carried on.

'I live in Woodston with my mum.'

More blushing.

'I mean my adopted mum.'

This was harder than I'd thought, but she smiled encouragingly at me as if she understood my difficulties.

'It's just the two of us,' I continued. 'I'm an only child, I mean. Mum and Dad didn't adopt any other children. And then my dad died when I was four, and since then it's just been me and Mum.'

Juju interrupted.

'Oh, my poor baby. How perfectly horrible for you. It must have been terribly difficult.'

'It was for Mum, I think. I can hardly remember when Dad was alive, so it's not so bad for me. I go to Thomas Peterson High, and my best friend is called Lydia. That's where I'm supposed to be this afternoon, with Lydia.'

'You mean your mother doesn't know that you've come to see me?' she said, but she didn't look cross or anything.

'No,' I said, blushing for the third time as I thought of Mum and the secret and letting her down that morning. 'I thought I'd find you and work it all out here first, and then I'd tell Mum. Is that OK with you?'

It hadn't crossed my mind that Juju might want me to tell Mum.

'That's fine. I can keep our little secret,' she said, and she winked at me.

I didn't really have anything else to say. I mean, that was me in a nutshell. So I went quiet and she just sat and looked at me for a while without saying anything either.

'I've thought about you, you know, over the years,' she began. She reached out to touch me but seemed to think better of it and pulled her hand back and rested it on her lap. 'I've wondered what you looked like, how you were getting on. I'm not allowed to contact you, you know. I had to wait to see if you wanted to get in touch with me. But I've thought about you each year on your birthday. August the second, isn't it? You see, I haven't forgotten. And here you are in my apartment. I can't quite believe it, darling. It's just perfect. So tell me, what do you do when you're not at school?'

And so I started to talk. It was a bit awkward at first, but she was so encouraging and she laughed when I said anything funny and she seemed so interested in everything that soon I was telling her all sorts of stuff. I told her about school and about Mrs Marshall and her messy flat and her brilliant cakes and Merlin. Then I told her about Lydia and how we have been best friends forever. Then I told her about the Bell twins and how they had been trying to steal Lydia from me, and she nodded sympathetically as if she completely understood about how difficult it is to be nearly a teenager, and I thought, as I was talking, how right I was to come and find her and how she was going to be able to help to make things better.

'Actually, it's been a bit tricky lately,' I started.

I slowed down a bit, as I was getting to the important bit and I wanted to make sure that Juju completely understood how difficult Mum was making my life by not letting me go to things. I needn't have worried.

'It sounds dreadful,' she said. 'Imagine your mother not letting you go to the fair, even though all your friends were going and your best friend was under attack from those awful twins? Oh, my poor baby.'

Then she reached out again, and this time she touched my hair with her manicured hand, and I felt very safe somehow, as if it was the most natural thing in the world. She started stroking me like a cat. It was all I could do not to purr. I could see her grey eyes just taking me in like she had never seen a girl before. Her eyes were cool, like the sea on a winter's day.

I felt I needed to defend Mum a bit. I didn't want Juju to get the wrong idea about her, so I added, 'Well, we always go together, Mum and me. I expect that she was disappointed that I wanted to go with my friends instead.'

'Hmmm,' said Juju in a disapproving tone. 'And did they all go without you, your so-called friends?'

So I told her all about what Lydia had told me about the fair, and then the next weekend when they had gone to see

*Espresso Dreams*without me, and Juju made sympathetic noises and carried on stroking my hair.

Our talking was interrupted by a new sound, and I looked up and saw an old-fashioned clock on the mantelpiece. It was striking four. I jumped. I felt a bit like Cinderella at midnight.

'I have to go,' I said quickly. 'I need to get back before Mum gets suspicious.'

I thought our meeting had gone really well, but I wanted it to be her that suggested we saw each other again rather than me. I needn't have worried.

'Oh, darling, must you go?' Juju said, her voice almost whining. 'We're having so much fun getting to know each other. I could chat to you for hours, but if you have to get back, then I understand. You must come again though. Soon.'

She gave my leg a gentle squeeze.

As I stepped out into the street to start my journey back home to Woodston, I realised that she hadn't told me a single thing about herself.

Chapter 13

Well, I got myself home with no problems, and by then Mum seemed to have forgotten about the missed shopping trip. She asked whether I'd had a nice time, and I said I had, and that was that. End of conversation. Of course, Mum didn't know that I'd just had the most exciting afternoon of my life and I couldn't tell her. Not yet. I wanted to get to know Juju a bit better before I filled Mum in. It had all gone really well, but I wasn't sure of my ground with Juju yet. She had certainly seemed sympathetic when I'd explained how Mum kept stopping me doing stuff that everyone else could do, but that didn't mean that she would be happy to help out herself. No. It was important that I knew what Juju thought before I told Mum that I'd found her, so I kept my mouth shut.

I did text Lydia though. I told her that it had all gone brilliantly, that Juju was lovely and her apartment (I'd noticed that she didn't call it a flat like we did) was incredibly posh. Lydia asked when I was going to see her again, but I just didn't know. That was going to be the tricky part, getting all the way to Juju's without Mum smelling a rat.

Anyway, the rest of my life was pretty dull that week until we got to Wednesday. That's when things started to heat up. I knew that Kyle's party was coming up fast. I could hardly not know, as it seemed to be all that anyone was talking about at school. All those on the guest list were busy showing off about it, talking about what they'd wear and their hair and stuff and all those who hadn't been invited were trying to look like they weren't bothered by being really off-hand about the whole thing. No one could quite believe that I was on the chosen list – neither could I really – but I pretended that it was the most obvious thing in the world that I should have been invited. I talked outfits and hair with Lydia whilst the speculation grew as to whether Louis would really come good with the beer. The number of people going seemed to be growing by the day, and pretty soon our invitation didn't feel that exclusive any more.

There was, however, one problem. I still hadn't cleared it with Mum. I wasn't sure how to play it. If I told her straight up that there was a birthday party and didn't mention that most of school seemed to be going or anything about alcohol, then I should be fine. After all, Mum wasn't a total witch, and even I was allowed to go to birthday parties. Or I could just say that I was going to a sleepover at Lydia's, and then there wouldn't be any talk of a party, and Mum would have nothing to object to. Of course, this would be a lie.

Lydia thought the second one was the best idea.

'I'll tell my Mum that you're sleeping over after the party, and then you can bring your stuff round and we can get ready at my house, and then your Mum need never know anything about it.'

I noticed that Lydia was going to tell her mum what was happening rather than ask her for permission.

'That might work,' I said doubtfully. 'As long as your mum doesn't mention anything to mine.'

'Well, why would she? They won't see each other, and the

main bit for your mum is that you are sleeping over at mine, and that's true. And this way there's no danger that your mum'll say no to the party.'

'But she might not say no though,' I said. 'And then I'd have lied for nothing.'

'Yes, but she might, and then what will you do?' argued Lydia, thumping me on the arm to make her point. 'You can't say you're coming for a sleepover then. She'll never believe you. Honestly, Kitty, it's the best plan. We get to go to the party and we get a sleepover afterwards so that we can talk about what happens all night. It's perfect.'

And it did seem perfect, so I let myself be talked into it. I felt bad but I wasn't exactly lying to Mum. I just wasn't telling her the whole truth. And it was her fault anyway for being so stupid about the fair and the film.

So I set it all up and I was pretty certain that Mum didn't suspect a thing.

When Saturday came, I folded my party clothes up really small and then wrapped my pyjamas round them so that Mum wouldn't spot them.

'I'm off now, Mum,' I shouted at the front door.

'Wait,' she shouted, and appeared from the lounge. My heart was beating so fast that I was sure she would hear it. 'Have you got everything? Toothbrush, phone, charger, clean underwear?'

'Yes! Honestly, Mum. I'm not six.'

'I know.'

She gave me a big hug and kissed me on the top of my head.

'Now, have a lovely time and do everything that Lydia's mum tells you. And be polite.'

'Yes. I will.'

We went through this palaver every time I went to anyone else's house.

'I shall be on my best behaviour and say please and thank you at every turn,' I said in my fake posh voice.

Mum ruffled my hair.

'I'll have less of your sarcasm, young lady! What time shall I expect you back tomorrow?'

'Around eleven?'

'OK. Ring me if there are any problems. I'll be just in watching the telly. Have a lovely time.'

'Bye!' I said, and left the flat.

Simple.

I walked round to Lydia's house to get ready. As her mum knew all about the party, there was no problem there. We put music on really loud and danced around while we got ready. That bit was almost as good as a party on its own, until Lydia's mum came to tell us to shut up because we were winding Callum up.

I was wearing my black, super-short skirt that Mum hated and a silvery top that I'd bought on our last shopping trip. It was a shame we hadn't been able to go to the shops on Saturday, because then I might have had something new to wear. Lydia had a new dress. It was really short too, with a sort of fitted top and a floaty skirt, and she had some sandals with heels on. She looked gorgeous with her long hair down her back and her tanned legs and everything. We put a bit of make-up on – not too much, because we didn't want Lydia's mum to notice that we were making a huge effort for just a regular party. When we were ready, Lydia snapped loads of photos of us on her phone. We thought we looked great. We were buzzing.

Around seven o'clock the doorbell rang and it was the Bell twins. I could see them turn their noses up at what I was wearing, even though they didn't look anything special themselves, but they did make a big fuss of Lydia, and rightly so. She looked fab.

So we set off for Kyle's party. He didn't live that far from Lydia, so it was an easy walk. As we got closer to his house, we could hear the music blasting out, and I remembered that someone had said he was going to borrow a sound system from a mate of his brother's. He obviously had because it was incredibly loud, and the nearer we got, the more excited and nervous I felt.

'Let's stick together,' said Lydia. 'That way we've always got someone to talk to and we won't get left on our own.'

I didn't want to have to stick with the Bell twins all night, but it made sense for us to stay as a group, at least until we worked the party out. However, I needn't have worried, because within two minutes of us arriving at the house, Chloe and Jess had gone off in search of some boy they fancied, leaving me and Lydia to chill in the kitchen. The door to the back yard was open, and people were spilling out there as it was still warm outside. Lydia and I helped ourselves to a can of coke each and set about analysing what everyone was wearing.

There were loads of people there, far more than I thought had been invited, and suddenly it didn't feel like such an exclusive party after all. Lots of them were from school, but there were plenty of people that I didn't recognise too. At one point Lydia pointed urgently to the back of someone's head as they passed by, and whispered, 'That's Louis. Kyle's brother.'

He was taller than Kyle and broader, and he was wearing jeans and a grey T-shirt. When he turned round, I could see that he had a cigarette drooping from his lips. Then he disappeared into the crowd and we went back to our people-watching, but a little bit later, he came back, and this time he headed straight for us. He had two bottles of beer in one hand and another cigarette in the other.

'Hi, girls,' he said. 'Having a good time?'

He spoke to us both, but he was staring at Lydia, which was no surprise, looking like she did.

'Yes, thanks. Are you Louis? Kyle said you did the playlist. It's awesome,' said Lydia.

I was surprised by how confident she sounded. If I'd had to talk to a seventeen-year-old boy, I wouldn't have known where to start. My words would have got all twisted up and I'd have blushed like an idiot, but Lydia was cool as a cucumber.

'Yeah. Do you like it? I've got another one a bit like this, and then something a bit quieter for later on when the sun goes down and the party proper starts.'

I wasn't sure what he meant. As far as I knew, the party finished at nine thirty, which was when Lydia's mum was coming to pick us up. It would still be light by then. Lydia didn't bat an eyelid. Well, she did, but only as she looked at Kyle from underneath her eyelashes. Where had she learned to do that?

'Want one of these?' he asked, and offered her one of the bottles.

'Ta,' she said, and took a huge gulp.

This surprised me too. I'd had a taste of beer and wine at Christmas, but I thought they were horrible and I couldn't imagine why anyone would drink them for pleasure. I was pretty certain that Lydia had never had beer before either, but she was doing a good impression of someone who drank it regularly. She was having another gulp. I didn't know much about drinking, but I did know that you weren't supposed to do it quickly. I tried to warn her, widening my eyes at her, but she didn't see me on purpose and kept staring at Louis. Louis didn't seem that interested, to be honest. He looked over Lydia's shoulder to a group of girls who were standing in the hallway, and then he said, 'Catch you later,' and moved off to talk to them.

As soon as he was out of earshot, I said, 'What are you doing? We're too young to drink beer! Your mum will go mental if she finds out. I didn't even know you liked beer.'

'I don't really. It's got a really funny taste, but it's fizzy and it's not that bad.'

She took another gulp and then pulled a face as she swallowed it.

'I wonder when you start to feel drunk. I don't feel anything yet.'

'I think it takes more than one bottle,' I said confidently, even though I didn't really have the first idea. 'Come on. Let's go and see what's going on in the other room.'

I put my empty Coke can down on the kitchen surface and pulled her towards the door. She followed me a little reluctantly, turning round to see if she could locate Louis, who had now moved back into the kitchen.

'Let's stay in here,' she whispered. She obviously wanted to try to talk to him again.

'Well, I need a wee,' I said. 'You stay here while I go and find the loo, and then I'll come straight back.'

She nodded her agreement and I went out into the hall towards the stairs. There were people sitting on the stairs, and I had to try hard not to step on them as I went past. At the top, Justine Barrow and Harry Smith were snogging. They'd been going out together forever, but it was still gross and I sneaked by as quickly as I could.

I found the bathroom. It was really messy with clothes over the floor and the contents of a cupboard spewing out everywhere. There wasn't even a holder for the loo roll. It was just balanced on the side of the bath. After I'd had a wee, I went to wash my hands, but there was no soap and the basin was full of toothpaste that someone had spat out but not washed away. It made me feel a bit queasy, so I didn't bother and hurried back downstairs to find Lydia.

I got back to the kitchen and, surprise, surprise, she was talking to Kyle's brother again and she had another bottle of beer in her hand. She was sitting on the edge of the table, and Louis was standing right next to her between her legs. She was laughing at something he'd said and kept flicking her hair and using it like a curtain to cover her mouth. I went and stood next to her, but she said hello and then ignored me and carried on listening to some story that Louis was telling her about a friend of his who had just got his first car. I didn't like the way things were going but I was stuck. I couldn't go home by myself, and I didn't fancy spending the whole party listening to Louis banging on to Lydia.

'I'm going to find Jess and Chlo,' I said, but I don't think Lydia even heard me.

Chloe and Jess were in the lounge dancing. The main light had been turned off, and there was a flashing disco globe thing and a strobe that made everyone look like they were in a cartoon. I danced over to where they were and they opened up a space for me. We had such a laugh mucking about to all the songs that came on. Actually, they can be quite good fun when you get to know them, and not nearly as bad as I'd thought. Anyway, we must have been dancing for nearly an hour with Kyle and a few of his mates, but then the playlist ran out and the music stopped, so I decided that I'd better go and find Lydia, as it must have been about time for her mum to come and get us.

I couldn't see her when I went into the kitchen. She wasn't sitting on the table any more and there was no sign of Louis. The room was really full and it smelled of hot bodies. I struggled to push my way through but I couldn't see Lydia anywhere. She had disappeared. Then some lad from Lydia's class shouted to me.

'Are you looking for your mate? I think she went outside.'

I wormed my way to the back door and then I finally found her. She was sitting on a box with her head between her legs. Her skirt was up round her waist, and her legs were all splayed out like Bambi.

'Lydia!' I shouted, and she looked up, but she couldn't seem to work out where my voice was coming from.

'Are you OK?' I asked.

She was grinning at me like an idiot.

'I'm fine,' she said in a sing-songy voice. 'Where's Louis gone? He's luuuvely. He went to find me a drink but he didn't come back.'

'I don't know where he is,' I said. 'We need to get ready to go. What time's your mum coming?'

'I don't know. Let me just find Louis and then I'll have another drink and then we'll ring Mum.'

She lurched forward to stand up but seemed to be having trouble.

'Oops!' she said. 'I feel a bit dizzy.'

And then, as she stood, all the colour drained from her face.

'I think I'm going to be …'
And then she threw up all over me.

Chapter 14

The sick was all liquid. We hadn't had any tea, assuming, wrongly as it turned out, that there would be food at the party. It didn't smell like sick usually smells either. It was a bit like the whiff you get when you walk past an open pub door. It was still pretty gross though, and it was all over my feet and the bottom of my legs. Lydia had sat back down and was crying, although I wasn't sure why, or how that would help.

'We'd better ring your mum and tell her to come and get us,' I said, but Lydia grabbed wildly at my legs and said in a slurry voice, 'No! You can't ring Mum. She'll kill me. What if I'm sick again? What if I'm sick in her car? You mustn't ring her. Promise me you won't ring her.'

Then she started retching, although not much sick came out this time.

'Well, we can't stay here,' I reasoned.

I checked the time on my phone.

'It's nearly ten o'clock. Won't she be wondering where we've got to?'

'She won't care. She'll be watching some rubbish on the telly and have forgotten us,' she said through the curtain of her hair, which was covering her face and dangling precariously close to the sick.

I found this strange about Lydia's mum. If I was out of the house, I knew Mum would be watching the clock until it was time for me to come home again. My mum would certainly never have let me go out on as loose an arrangement as this.

All around me the party was still rocking, although I noticed that the guests were mainly Louis's age now. I couldn't see anyone who I recognised and definitely no one that I felt I could ask for help. Lydia was now lying down on the concrete patio and looked as if she would fall asleep, although from time to time, she did a little sob. At least she seemed to have stopped throwing up.

There was only one thing for it. I was going to have to ring Mum. It would mean that it would come out that I had lied to her about where I was and that I'd been at a party that she obviously wouldn't have approved of and that Lydia had been drinking and was sick. I shuddered at the thought of the amount of trouble I would be in. But what were the alternatives? Lydia was adamant that I shouldn't ring her mum, and we could hardly walk home. Resolutely I punched the number into my phone. Mum answered it almost straightaway.

'Kitty? Is that you? Is everything alright?'

'No, Mum, it's not. Lydia and me are at Kyle's birthday party, but Lydia's been drinking beer and she's been sick all over everything, including me. She says I'm not allowed to ring her mum, because she'll be in trouble, but I don't know how we are going to get home, and so I didn't know what to do. She's sort of asleep now.'

'Where are Kyle's parents?' Mum asked urgently.

'They're not here. His brother Louis was here. He's seventeen but I don't know where he is. Most of our friends seem to have gone home. It's mainly Louis's friends here now.'

'I'll come straightaway,' Mum said in her calmest voice, and I felt reassured that she would make it all better the way she always does.

I gave her the address as best as I could remember it, and a description of the house, and then I sat on the concrete slabs, rested Lydia's tear-stained and sicky head on my lap and stroked her matted hair.

It wasn't long before I heard Mum's voice in the hallway. She wasn't shouting, just asking to be let through. I called out to her but I didn't stand up, because I didn't want to disturb Lydia, who was deeply asleep.

Mum came out of the back door and rushed straight to us.

'Oh, Kitty. Are you OK? What on earth are you doing here? You must never lie to me about where you are. Anything could have happened to you and I'd have had no idea how to find you. I thought you were tucked up safe at Lydia's.'

She squeezed my head, it being the only bit of me that she could get to with Lydia sprawled all over the place.

'Right. We'll talk about this later. The main thing now is to get Lydia home. How much has she had to drink?'

'I don't know. I saw her have two beers but then I was dancing for a bit, and when I came to find her, she was drunk and then she threw up and started crying.'

'How long has she been asleep?'

'Not long, I don't think. Ten minutes maybe.'

'OK. We need to wake her up and get her to stand up so I can judge how bad she is.'

Mum leant forward and started patting Lydia on the cheek. When Lydia didn't respond, Mum hit her a bit harder, and that brought Lydia round. She groaned and opened her eyes a bit.

'Just let me sleep, will you?' she said, and was closing her eyes

93

again but Mum was pulling her to her feet.

'Not yet, Lydia. You have to wake up for a bit so that we can get you home, and then you can go to bed.'

Lydia was still groaning but Mum made her stand, and with Mum holding her under one armpit and me under the other, we managed to get her sort of staggering across the yard and back into the kitchen. People moved out of the way to let us through, but nobody asked if Lydia was OK or if they could help. We made it to the front door and out into the street. Mum's car was parked right outside. She unlocked it, and we manhandled Lydia into the front seat and put her seat belt on. Then Mum opened the window as far as it would go and we set off to Lydia's house.

'Do you think she'll be OK, Mum?' I asked, although I hardly dared speak, as it was obvious that Mum was really cross.

'I hope so, Kathryn, but honestly, what did you think you were doing? And what was Cheryl thinking letting you go in the first place? You're twelve years old.'

She emphasised each individual word as she spat them out. It took no time to get to Lydia's. Mum stopped the car and went round to get her out.

'You stay there,' she said, and then had second thoughts. 'No. You come with me. You need to get your sleepover stuff. I assume you have got some sleepover stuff and that bit wasn't a lie too.'

I nodded my head and tried to look as sorry as I possibly could.

'Right. Come and give me a hand with Lydia.'

Lydia had fallen asleep again during the brief journey home. Mum shook her awake and this time she didn't even pretend to be gentle.

'Come on, young lady. Let's see what your mother has got to say.'

If I hadn't been so scared about how much trouble I was going to be in, I would have almost been enjoying this, my mum being tough and in control. She had a fire in her eyes that I hadn't seen before, and she looked determined and dangerous.

We dragged Lydia to the front door, and Mum rang the doorbell. A light flicked on in the hallway, and then Cheryl appeared through the frosted glass. She opened the door and looked at me and Mum and the crumpled heap between us that was Lydia.

'Oh my God!' she said, pushing back Lydia's no-longer-lovely locks so that she could see her face. 'What on earth has happened? Lydia, my princess …'

Lydia opened her eyes, tried to focus on her mum and started crying again.

'I'm so sorry. I'm sorry. I'm so sorry,' she kept saying over and over again.

'I think she's had some beer at this party that they were at. I knew nothing about a party, but I gather that you were supposed to be picking them up?'

Although Mum wasn't shouting, I could hear how cross she was from the tone of her voice.

'Well, I was waiting for Lydia to ring and tell me that they were ready.'

'And did it not occur to you that they were out rather late?' Mum asked, staring straight at Lydia's mum.

'Well, I don't know. I must have lost track of time. How come you've collected them?'

'Lydia wouldn't let Kitty ring you, so Kitty did the sensible thing and rang me. I think Lydia is OK. No need for a stomach pump.'

That sounded absolutely hideous, whatever it was.

'She has vomited quite spectacularly, but now I think she just needs to sleep it off. Kitty,' she said, turning to me. 'Can you nip up and get your things, please?'

Lydia's mum looked a bit thrown by my mum inviting me into Lydia's house, but she couldn't really offer to get my stuff for me, as she was holding Lydia up.

'Yes, of course. Go get it all, Kitty,' she said, and I snuck past her and up the stairs.

I couldn't hear what they said when I was collecting all my bits and pieces together. It took a while because we'd been so excited when we were getting ready that we hadn't really tidied anything up. When I got back down, it was obvious that Mum and Lydia's mum had had words and there was a really horrible atmosphere between them.

'Right,' said Mum purposefully. 'Have you got everything, Kitty? We'll be off, then. Good night, Cheryl. I hope Lydia feels better soon.'

And with that, Mum turned and strode towards the car with me running after her, trying to keep up. I looked back as Mum was unlocking the car. Lydia's mum was just closing the door, but I heard her say, 'What have they done to you, my princess?' to Lydia, which seemed really unfair because, actually, Lydia had done it to herself.

Mum was very quiet in the car, and soon we were back on Fieldview Road. I grabbed my bag and we went in and up the stairs to our flat without saying a word. Once we were in with the door shut though, Mum turned, arms folded, and stared at me. I don't think I've ever seen her look so angry.

'Right, young lady. Would you like to tell me what that was

all about?'

So I told her. I told her all about getting invited accidentally to Kyle's party and how it made me feel great after I'd missed out on the fair and the film. I didn't overplay that. I could see Mum's hackles rising as soon as I mentioned them. And then I told her about the sleeping-over-at-Lydia's plan.

'You see,' Mum said, 'that's what I don't understand. Why did you have to lie about going to the party? I would have let you go. I would have picked you up much sooner than Cheryl seemed to think was appropriate, but I wouldn't have said no.'

I wanted to point out that she'd been saying no a lot more than she said yes recently, but I didn't. I didn't tell her it was Lydia's idea either. Lydia was in enough bother as it was.

'Unless, of course,' she carried on, 'you knew what kind of party it was going to be, and that I wouldn't approve.'

'I didn't, Mum. Honest. I knew it was a house party and that Kyle's brother was going to get a few beers …'

'You knew that there'd be alcohol there?' Mum interrupted. 'Well, that puts a whole different slant on it. No wonder you didn't want to tell me. You knew precisely what I'd say. Did you have any of this beer?'

I shook my head solemnly.

'Good. Well, at least you've still got some common sense, which is more than can be said for Lydia. Anything could have happened to her. She could have died. She could have got alcohol poisoning. She could have been attacked, with all those older boys there. They wouldn't care that you were only twelve once they had a drink inside them. Drink makes people do stupid things, Kitty, and until you're old enough to deal with the consequences of that, you must … not … touch it. Do you hear me?'

I nodded furiously.

'Lydia has been very lucky. No doubt she'll have a terrible hangover tomorrow, which will jolly well serve her right, but she should be fine. However, you, young lady, have let me down, and I'm very disappointed in you. You must not tell me you're in one place when you're actually somewhere else. Anything could have happened to you, and I wouldn't even have known that you were in any danger.'

'Lydia's mum knew where we were,' I interrupted, trying to show that I hadn't been entirely irresponsible.

At the mention of Lydia's mum, Mum just rolled her eyes.

'Well, a fat lot of good that did!' she scoffed.

I wondered whether she and Cheryl would ever be friends again, not that they were particularly, but you know what I mean.

'Kitty. Trust is absolutely fundamental to any relationship. If I can't trust you to tell the truth and be where you say you are, then it's going to be very difficult for me to let you have the freedoms that you clearly think you need. Do you understand that?'

I nodded.

'Right, then, it's been a long evening and I think we both need to go to bed. I'll consider your punishment overnight, but you needn't doubt that it will be a severe one. Good night, Kathryn.'

She kissed the top of my head and then headed to lock the front door and shut everything down for the night. I went into my room and closed the door quietly behind me.

Once I was in bed, I started to think about what Mum had said. I seemed to have got off quite lightly. At least she hadn't shouted at me. But what was there, nagging away at me, was what she said about trust, because, of course, the party wasn't the only thing that I had lied to her about. There was the whole Juju thing too.

Chapter 15

Well, I was grounded. It didn't really come as a shock, to be honest. The only question was going to be how long it would last. As it turned out, it was only for a week. I was quite surprised – I'd expected longer, but I got the impression from some catty things that Mum said the next day that she really blamed Lydia and Lydia's mum for what happened. This was a bit of a pain, as it was going to make it difficult if Mum didn't like Lydia any more, but at least it wasn't too long a time to be stuck at home.

Not much happened on the Sunday. I obviously couldn't go anywhere, so I tried to make it up to Mum by being really helpful around the flat. I cleaned the bathroom and my bedroom, and even offered to make tea, although Mum said she'd do it. I didn't hear anything from Lydia. I texted her but I didn't get a reply, so I decided that I'd just have to wait until Monday to see her at school.

There was no sign of her waiting for me at the junction on the way to school, so I walked on my own. When I got there, I couldn't find her either, but I overheard some Year 9s talking about her in the corridor. It seemed that everyone had heard that she'd got drunk and been sick at the party. I could see people turn to stare at me as I walked past as if, because I was

Lydia's friend, I was somehow guilty as well. Kyle was sitting in his usual place with his back against the radiator.

'Great party, eh, Kitty? And what about your mate Lydia? How was her head yesterday?'

I was pleased that Kyle assumed I'd know all the details of Lydia's hangover, but a bit upset by the fact that, actually, I didn't.

I mumbled something about it being a good night, but before he could quiz me further, our tutor came in and we had to be quiet. At break time, I went to look for Lydia and eventually found her with Chloe and Jess and a gaggle of other girls from her form all crowded round her.

'Hi,' I said as I approached. 'Are you feeling better, Lydia?'

I asked, but it was more because that was one of those things that you said rather than because I was expecting an answer. I knew she'd tell me all about everything when the others weren't there, so I was surprised by what came next.

'Like you care,' Lydia said, shrugging her shoulder and turning slightly away from me.

Her voice had a really nasty tone that I hadn't heard her use to me before. It shocked me and I didn't really know what to say.

'Of course I care,' I said, confused. 'What do you mean?'

'What I say,' said Lydia harshly, but she didn't look at me.

Something was seriously wrong here, but I couldn't for the life of me work out what it was. I tried again.

'I don't understand. Are you cross with me about something, because I don't know what I've done to make you?'

'Cross, she asks. Cross! Of course I'm cross. I can't believe that you even have the nerve to ask.'

Her lip curled as she spoke, and her lovely blue eyes were

101

dark and narrowed into slits. I started to feel really shaky. We'd had rows before. Of course we had, but nothing like this. Lydia was being really different, cold, offhand, like she really didn't want anything to do with me. The Bells and all those other girls were watching, waiting to see what I did next.

'Lydia, I really don't know what I've done to upset you. How about we go for a walk on our own …' I nodded my head at her little entourage. 'Away from that lot, and then we can talk about whatever it is that you think I've done.'

'I don't want to go for a walk with you. In fact, I don't want to go anywhere with you ever again. You can consider our friendship over, dead, terminated, kaput!'

Then, and this hurt as much as her words, she turned to the gang of girls, raised her eyebrows and smiled a really nasty smile at them, like her master plan was all going smoothly. I could feel the tears pricking in my eyes. Part of me wanted to turn around and run away from them all, but I needed to know what I was supposed to have done, and so I wiped my eyes dry with the back of my hand and asked again.

'I'm not going anywhere until you tell me what you're so upset about.'

I think I sounded much braver than I felt. I put my hands on my hips to show that I meant business.

Lydia stepped towards me, and the crowd of girls fell back to let her out.

'Well, let me see,' said Lydia.

Her voice was so twisted with hate that I barely recognised it. She held up her hand and started counting the list of things I'd done wrong on her fingers.

'Shall we start with you abandoning me at the party so that Louis could get me drunk and do God knows what to me?'

I was outraged.

'I didn't. You told me to go away. I was only in the other room dancing. Wasn't I, Chlo, Jess? We were there together. You told me to go away and so I did.'

I looked to the Bells for confirmation of my story. They knew that Lydia had sent me away so she could work on Louis, but they just shrugged their shoulders as if they had no memory of what I was saying.

'But we did,' I said again, appealing to the twins. 'You know we did. We were dancing with that strobe light thing in the lounge, and Lydia was in the kitchen.'

But they had decided to forget that, or at least not to back me up.

'Now,' continued Lydia, 'what else was there? Oh yes. I remember. Ringing your mummy like a good little girl to come and get you.'

'But you told me not to ring your mum. You begged me. What was I supposed to do? We couldn't stay there all night and you were in no state to do anything.'

I stopped. Lydia was glaring at me at the mention of her state. Obviously, that was going to be my fault too.

'But the worst of your crimes, and the one that means we can never more be friends, is that you spilled the beans to your mum. Friends are supposed to keep things secret. Not blab to their mummy at the first sign of trouble.'

I couldn't believe what I was hearing. Was all this just because I told Mum about the party? What was I supposed to do? I had to explain why we'd been there in the first place, and anyway, it was me that was grounded as a result, not her.

'Yes, little Kitty blabs to mummy, and then mummy picks up the phone and screams and shouts at my mum so that I get into even more trouble than I already was. My mum didn't need to know that there was alcohol at that party.'

My mouth fell open. I couldn't believe what I was hearing. Had she forgotten that we had had to carry her home, that she had been sick everywhere and cried like a baby? How was her mum going to miss the fact that there was alcohol at the party in the face of massive clues like that?

'But, Lydia,' I protested, 'you were paralytic.'

I could see a smirk pass round Lydia's gang of supporters. They were obviously enjoying this.

'How could your mum possibly not have noticed the state you were in? We had to carry you, for goodness' sake.'

'Well, I wish you'd just left me there. I was perfectly fine. But no. You had to ring mummy and land me in massive trouble. Well, that's it!' she continued, now so close to me that a little bit of her spit landed on my cheek. 'We're finished. You are no longer my friend. I want absolutely nothing to do with you as long as I live.'

She stood there, sticking one hip forward, and sneered at me. I took one last look at her, and then I turned and ran away from them as fast as I could, and I didn't stop running until I got to the girls' loo, where I found myself an empty cubicle and locked myself in. Tears streamed down my face. I was embarrassed and humiliated, but most of all, I was shocked that Lydia could speak to me like that after all those years. I sat on the loo and cried and cried until the bell rang.

Chapter 16

I didn't see Lydia for the rest of the day, which was probably a good thing. I needed time to think through what she'd said. Mum must have rung Cheryl after I'd gone to bed, because if she'd done it the next day, I would surely have heard her. Then Cheryl must have shouted at Lydia, and somehow the whole horrible mess ended up being my fault. The more I thought about it, the larger the enormous rock that seemed to be lodged right in the middle of me grew.

What was worse, I had absolutely no idea how to make it better. Lydia was crosser than I'd ever seen her before. I certainly couldn't talk to her today. Maybe, I thought, she might calm down by tomorrow and we could get over this and move on. But then I remembered the sneer and that awful voice that she used, and I knew that our friendship was totally over. I couldn't see any way back, and when I thought about that, the tears would start welling up in my eyes. Even my chemistry teacher asked me if something was wrong, and he wouldn't notice if a small army marched through his lesson backwards, singing the national anthem.

The end of the day couldn't have come quickly enough, and when the last bell went, I packed my bag and virtually ran from the classroom and out of school. I didn't want to bump into

Lydia. I didn't want to bump into anyone. I just wanted to get home and close the door on them all.

When Mum got back, I was sitting on the sofa. The TV was on but I wasn't really watching it.

'Good day?' asked Mum as she came into the room.

She dropped her bag on the table and then came and flopped down next to me and kicked her shoes off.

'My feet are killing me. I need some old-lady shoes. I know I said I never would, but now I'm not sure ... Are you OK, sweetheart?'

She looked at me and reached out to grab my hand. I had intended to play it cool with Mum. After all, this mess was partly her fault, but when it came down to it, I just couldn't. Tears started pouring down my cheeks again.

'Oh, Mum. Everything is such a mess.'

'Why? What's happened?'

She twisted herself round on the sofa so she could look straight at me and took my other hand between both of hers.

'Lydia's not speaking to me.'

'Oh, is that all?' she said lightly, like she was almost laughing at me. 'Well, we've been here before, haven't we? She'll get over it. She always does. You just need to show her that you're not bothered and spend some time with your other friends until she forgets that she's fallen out with you.'

'No,' I said. 'You don't understand. This time it's different. She says our friendship is dead and she never wants to have anything to do with me ever again.'

'And is this all to do with what happened on Saturday night?'

'Kind of,' I said cagily, reluctant to tell her that what she had done was ruining my life. Again. But Mum was having none of it.

'What do you mean, kind of?'

'Well,' I started tentatively. 'She's cross because she says that I abandoned her at the party.'

'That's rich considering that if it wasn't for you, she might still be there.'

'And she's cross because I rang you to come and get us, because then her mum had to find out, but she begged me not to ring her mum and I didn't know what else to do.'

'You did exactly the right thing, Kitty. One of the reasons why children shouldn't drink is because they don't have enough life experience to deal with the consequences. Lydia is far too young for alcohol. I blame Kyle's brother, Louis, is it? And his parents, of course. But also I blame Lydia. What she did was silly and irresponsible, and being angry with you about it rather than facing up to take the blame herself just shows how immature she is.'

I could tell that Mum was still cross with Lydia. Her voice was getting higher and higher as she spoke, but this had a weird effect on me. Instead of being grateful to Mum for taking my side, I found myself wanting to defend Lydia.

'She's not immature!' I said, louder than I'd meant to.

Mum raised her eyebrows at me and let go of my hands.

'Well, I wouldn't call going to a stranger's house and then getting so drunk that you can't stand up terribly mature behaviour. She put herself and you in huge danger by her stupidity. I know you think you're all grown up and can do what you like, but really, you're still children, and that's how you'll be treated until you can show that you know how to behave.'

My stomach was getting tight as she spoke, and I could feel my heart starting to beat faster. I hadn't been cross with her when we started this conversation, but I was now. Suddenly I couldn't hold it all in any more, and all my shame and hurt and anger came rushing out.

'Well, it's all your fault anyway,' I shouted at her. 'Why did you have to go and ring Lydia's mum like that? It just made everything so much worse.'

Mum looked a bit taken aback but she carried on regardless.

'I rang Cheryl because I wanted her to know how disappointed I was with her, and how irresponsible I thought she had been with the most precious thing in my life – you. If she chooses to take offence, then that's up to her, but I'm sure she knows that she is partly to blame for this.'

'How? How can she possibly be to blame for this? All she did was say that we could go to a party, which is what normal mums say, and then offer to come and get us afterwards. How can you say that it's her fault?'

'She should have asked more questions. She should have found out what kind of party it was, and made a proper arrangement for picking you up. You could have been anywhere. It was lazy parenting to just let you go off like that, and I told her so.'

'Well, I wish you hadn't, because now not only do I have no social life because my mother won't let me out of the house, but I also have no best friend and am the laughing stock of the entire school, so thanks for that, Mum. Thanks a bunch!'

I wriggled free and stormed out of the room, giving the door a huge bang as I went. Who cared about Mrs Marshall and her nosing into our lives?

'You come back here right now, young lady, and apologise,' I heard Mum shout behind me, but I ignored her and went straight to my room, slamming that door too for good measure.

I was too cross to cry, so I threw myself down on my bed and stared up at the ceiling. This mess was all Mum's fault. If she hadn't rung Cheryl, none of it would have happened, Lydia and I would still be best friends, and no doubt, we would be laughing about the party and Louis and all of it.

As I lay there fuming, a text landed. I assumed it would be from Lydia – they usually were – and then I remembered that Lydia would probably never text me ever again. Mildly curious, I reached my phone out from my blazer pocket and looked at the screen. It was from Juju. In all the chaos of the last couple of days, I had completely forgotten about her even though it was only just over a week since I'd made my trip across town. I pressed 'Read'.

Hi sweet pea. Just checking that you got home again safe. Loved meeting you. Can we do it again soon? Juju xxx

I cringed a little that I had forgotten to let her know that I had got home OK, but so much had happened since then. Immediately I started to type a reply, and then I stopped. What was I going to say? I was grounded, so that was next weekend out, and now that I wasn't friends with Lydia, how on earth was I going to manufacture enough time to get over there to see her? I would need to come up with a really clever plan.

Hi Juju. I got back fine thanks. Would love to see you again but not sure when. Can I let you know when I've worked something out? Thanks Kitty xxx

Whatever happened, I wasn't going to let this whole mess spoil what I had started with Juju. In fact, if anything, I was going to need her even more after this. I could hear Mum moving around in the flat. Any minute now she would come and tap on my door and try to make things up with me, but I wasn't ready to make things up with her. The phone beeped again.

That's fine sweet pea. Make it soon. I miss you. J xxx

She missed me. Mum was making my life hell, but Juju missed me. It made me feel special, loved. I was definitely right to go and find her. Next time I saw her, I was going to explain what I needed her to do to help.

There was a knock on my door.

'Kitty, I'm going to start on tea now. Is there anything you fancy?'

I could tell that she was making an effort, but I just wasn't in the mood.

'I don't care,' I replied without making any effort to sound interested. 'Whatever.'

'Oh. OK.' Mum's voice was brisk, her white flag having been rejected. 'Well, it will be ready in half an hour or so. You'd better get on with your homework.'

Then I heard her walking away from my door. I was still quite cross with her, although it had begun to fade, especially after I got the text from Juju. Somehow I was going to have to come up with a new plan. I wondered whether Juju could come to Woodston and we could meet in a cafe somewhere, but I rejected that idea pretty quickly. I wasn't ready to have her here where anyone might see her and start asking questions. After all, she was my secret. Well, mine and Lydia's. A cold shiver suddenly blew over me but I brushed it away. Lydia knew how important this was to me. She would never do anything to wreck it, no matter what had had happened between us. Would she?

Chapter 17

The rest of the week was truly terrible. Lydia was still going out of her way to make me feel bad. I kept hoping she'd get bored and move on to just ignoring me, but no. Whenever she got a chance, she'd make some nasty comment about me ringing Mum to come and rescue us. I could hear her shout out as I walked past, and then the gaggle of girls around her would collapse into laughter. It was horrible, and as much as I tried to just ignore her, it really hurt that someone I thought was my best friend for life could be so vile.

The torture at school made things pretty difficult at home too. I suppose I knew that it wasn't actually Mum's fault and I was being unfair by blaming her, but at the same time, I had to channel my anger somewhere, and there was nowhere else for it to go. So I was monosyllabic. Mum kept trying to engage me in conversation, asking me about school, and when that didn't work, trying to work up some excitement about my favourite TV shows, but I was resolutely uncooperative. If I was suffering, then she could jolly well suffer too. I was even rude to Mrs Marshall. I felt bad about that, but now I knew that she was just acting as Mum's spy, I said as little to her as I could get away with.

I had no one. I was completely alone. Apart from Juju, of

course. So I focused my energies on trying to devise a plan to get to see her. So far I'd come up with nothing. Without Lydia to provide my cover story, I was stuck. Plus there was the added problem of me being grounded. I needed to think of something that meant I didn't have to rely on anyone else helping me, and it had to be something that Mum would approve of.

Then I had a spectacular idea. Posters had started appearing around school for the end-of-year play. The drama department often put on shows, and I had never been that interested before, but this time I wondered if it might not be the perfect cover.

After school that night, I began a conversation with Mum. I think she was so delighted that I was saying something more than 'yes' or 'no' that she gave me her undivided attention, and I did my best acting to lure her in, which was very appropriate in the circumstances.

'Did you know that they do a play at school at the end of the year?' I asked innocently.

'No. That sounds fun,' said Mum with a smile as she tried to engage me. 'Can anybody be in it?'

'Yes. I'm thinking I might audition.'

Mum looked slightly taken aback. I don't think she had ever pictured me on a stage.

'Well,' she said, recovering herself fast, 'I think that would be a lovely idea. What's the play?'

Damn. I should have done my research a bit better.

'I'm not sure,' I said weakly. 'I think they'll tell us that later but I know it's a musical. And I can sing, can't I?'

Mum frowned, and I started to lose my nerve a bit until I remembered that, as this was all a scam, it didn't matter whether I could sing or not.

'Well, yes. I suppose so,' she said. 'Do you think you can sing in front of a room full of people rather than just in the shower?'

'I don't know,' I said. 'But if I don't try …'

'Well, good for you,' she said with a smile, her doubts forgotten. 'I think it's an excellent plan. I'm proud of you.'

She gave me a little squeeze around my shoulders.

I was on a roll now. This acting thing was a breeze.

'I was thinking that after all that stuff with Lydia, I need some new friends. This might be a great way of meeting people.'

Mum was nodding enthusiastically. I could see the thought *get her away from Lydia* racing through her mind. I ignored it and continued.

'There's only one problem.'

'Oh?'

'Well …' I began slowly with a sigh. 'I can't go to the auditions, can I?'

'Why not?'

'They're on Saturday and I'm still grounded.'

My killer point! I let it hang in the air between us and tried to look a bit downhearted without going over the top.

'I think we can overlook the grounding thing for something like this,' said Mum, as I'd known she would. 'It's almost over anyway and you have been really good all week.'

This last point was a blatant lie. I'd been a nightmare all week and we both knew it.

'What time is the audition?' Mum asked.

'We have to be at school for one o'clock, and then I think it'll take all afternoon until around five. Would that be OK?'

'Yes. I'm not going to be so petty-minded as to enforce a punishment when it means you missing out on a fantastic opportunity like this. You should go. You never know, you may get a big part.'

'Yes, maybe,' I said wistfully. 'I need to sing a song, and then they'll give us something to work on all afternoon, like a workshop thing, and then they'll pick at the end of the session.'

'What will you sing?'

This was going like a dream. I'd planned it all out, and the lies were just tripping off my tongue.

'I thought I'd do 'Somewhere over the Rainbow'. I already know all the words, so I just have to work on my performance.'

'Great idea. That's a lovely song. How exciting! Wouldn't it be great if you got a part? I'd love to come and see you performing on a stage.'

I smiled as enthusiastically as I could manage. Of course, that was the fundamental flaw in my plan. If I used all the rehearsal times for seeing Juju, then I wouldn't be on a stage at the end, but I'd decided that I would cross that bridge when I came to it. For the time being, the show gave me the perfect cover. Mum would never suspect, and I would be able to get to see Juju whenever I liked.

'Right, then. I better go and start practising,' I said.

'Good for you,' Mum said. 'Well done, Kitty Cat.'

I felt a twinge of guilt, but I pushed it to the back of my mind and walked off to my room, singing the opening lines of my audition piece as I went. As soon as I got to my room, I texted Juju.

Hi. I have a plan. I can be at yours for around 2 on Saturday if that's OK with you. K xxx

The reply came back quickly.

That's perfect. Can't wait to see you. J xxx

114

Chapter 18

By the time Saturday came, I could sing 'Somewhere over the Rainbow' like a pro. I was pretty certain that I would have got a part – if I'd actually been auditioning, that is. It was a shame really, because the more I pretended that I was going to audition, the more I actually fancied having a go. But that couldn't be helped. I had to keep reminding myself of the bigger picture.

I did my homework and helped Mum around the flat in the morning, and then the time arrived for me to head to school for the audition workshop. I think Mum was a bit nervous for me. She was flapping round me like she does when I have to do something important, fiddling with my clothes and asking loads of pointless questions. When I'd got my bag and stuff ready, I went to tell her that I was going. She gave me a big hug.

'Well, good luck, Kitty Cat,' she said. 'No, wait. I'm not supposed to say that, am I? They say "break a leg" in the theatre, don't they?'

'Do they?' I said, pulling a face as I wondered how breaking a leg could ever be considered to be good luck. 'That doesn't sound very encouraging.'

'It's bad luck to say good luck. And breaking a leg is

something to do with the number of curtain calls you get, I think,' she replied, laughing at herself. 'Well, whatever it is, I hope it goes really well. And you'll be back around five?'

'Yes, but it might run over, so don't worry if I'm a little bit late.'

This was perfect. I was a genius for coming up with something as fool-proof as this.

I skipped down the stairs and over the road towards school. I would need to double back on myself to get to the station, but Mum wouldn't see that. I was home and dry.

The trip to Juju's apartment was much easier second time around. I wasn't nervous at all this time, and I even enjoyed watching all the other people as I travelled. It didn't take long either. The connections worked really well, and I was turning into Juju's road about fifteen minutes early. I breezed along the pavement as if I lived there myself. I could hear some children laughing in the garden in the centre of the square, and I let myself have a little fantasy daydream about living here with Mum and Juju. It wasn't that hard to imagine really.

As I approached the door, I saw that there was someone coming out of number forty-eight, so I held back a bit. It was an old man – well, older than Mum anyway. He was dressed in a navy-blue suit with a blue-and-white striped shirt underneath, and he had really shiny shoes on. He looked pretty rich, I thought. He came out of the front door and then walked a few steps in the other direction from me. I was just thinking that there were lots of apartments in the building, when he stopped, turned and looked back up at Juju's window on the top floor. He didn't wave or anything, but something made me think that that was where he'd come from. I looked up but I couldn't see whether Juju was at the window or not.

As I went in through the big black door and made my way to the intercom, I wondered about the man. A boyfriend maybe? I didn't think she was married. Maybe he was just a friend, or something to do with work? As I thought this, I realised that I didn't know what Juju did. It was obviously a really highly paid job for her to be able to afford to live here and buy those gorgeous clothes. As I pushed the top button, I thought that I should try and learn a little bit more about my birth mother. Almost straightaway I heard Juju's voice on the other end of the intercom.

'Did you forget something, big boy? Do you need to pop back up? I can help you look for it.'

I didn't know what to say, so I just said, 'Hi. It's me. Kitty.'

There was the slightest pause, and then she said, 'Kitty darling. Hi. You're early. How marvellous. Come on up and I'll open the door.'

I headed up in the now familiar lift, and when I reached the top floor, Juju was waiting for me. Even though it was past lunchtime, she was wearing a silky cream dressing gown and not much underneath as far as I could tell. It threw me a bit.

'Oh. I'm sorry. Were you asleep? You're not ill, are you? Do you want me to go?'

I asked the question because I thought that was polite, but I was desperate for her to say no.

'Of course not, darling. Come on in. I've been waiting for you. I'm just having a lazy Saturday lie-in and I haven't got round to getting dressed yet. Go to the kitchen and find yourself a drink whilst I throw some clothes on.'

She gestured to a door that I hadn't noticed the first time I'd been in the apartment.

I opened it slowly, like there was something dangerous

behind it, and walked into a huge kitchen. Everything was incredibly modern and it was almost totally white – the floor, the cupboard doors, even the work surfaces. The only splashes of colour came from the fridge and the kettle, which were both postbox red. There was absolutely nothing out of place. No piles of post waiting to be dealt with, no stray plastic carrier bags balled up on the side, no washing-up, not even a toaster. When I looked a bit more closely, I began to wonder whether anyone actually ever cooked in this kitchen. It was all so shiny and clean that it was hard to picture a pan of potatoes boiling away on the hob, or a packet of bacon under the grill. Was there even a cooker? I found it eventually, all sleek and slimline, hidden away in one of the cupboards. I wasn't sure I was going to learn much about Juju from in here.

She had told me to get a drink, so I opened the fridge. That was sparkling too, which was hardly surprising. There was no food in it – well, almost none. Certainly nothing fresh anyway. There were a couple of jars towards the back of the top shelf, and there was some milk and a packet of coffee beans in the door. The fridge wasn't empty though. Every shelf was full of drinks. The first two had bottles of champagne on them. I could tell what it was because I recognised the gold foil caps. Then there was a shelf that just had little green bottles of beer, like the ones that Louis had given Lydia. The next shelf had bottles of wine and a bright blue, square-shaped bottle that I thought was gin. The last shelf had cans and cartons of fruit juice. The door was full of water.

I helped myself to a can of Coke, and I was just shutting the fridge door when Juju reappeared. She had put on a pair of jeans and a big, sloppy blue jumper, and her feet were bare, showing her perfect red toenails.

'So, how are you, sweet pea?'

'I'm fine,' I lied. 'How are you?'

'I'm good too, thank you. Shall we go and sit down?'

She led the way to the lounge and flopped down on one of the big sofas and then tapped the cushion next to her. I felt a bit nervous again, and I must have been biting my lip, because she said, 'Don't be worried, darling. I'm not going to eat you. I just want to get to know you a bit better. Something tells me you're not quite as happy as you were last time I saw you. What's happened?'

I didn't mean to tell her. I had decided before I arrived that I was going to keep my mouth shut about my horrible week, but it suddenly felt the most natural thing in the world to be telling her my problems. So I let it all come gushing out. The party, and Lydia deciding that she hated me, and Mum grounding me, and all of it. Last of all, I told her, with not a little pride, about my clever plan to get my passes out to visit her.

'And won't your mother smell a rat when you spend all this time rehearsing and she never gets to see the show?'

I grinned at her.

'That's the hole in my plan,' I laughed. 'But I'll cross that bridge and all that. Perhaps I can get sacked from the cast at the eleventh hour or come down with tonsillitis. Or perhaps I will have told her all about you by then, so it won't matter.'

I watched her reaction carefully as I said this. I wasn't really joking. I didn't like having to do all this sneaking about, and anyway, how was Juju going to go about helping Mum with bringing me up if they never actually met? I couldn't read her face though. I had no idea what she was thinking. She certainly didn't give much away.

Suddenly she stood up, almost making me spill my Coke on

the pale sofa.

'Let's go out!' she said. 'I haven't been shopping for ages. We can treat ourselves to a proper girly afternoon.'

Quickly I checked my watch, but it was only two twenty. I had bags of time before I had to start for home.

'OK,' I replied. 'Where shall we go?'

I stood up too, but as I did so, my ancient phone slipped out of my jeans pocket. I went to grab it, but Juju was quicker, and she snatched it up and began examining it. My cheeks burned with shame. It really was a rubbish phone. Juju seemed to think so too.

'What is this?' she asked, although I could hear exactly what she thought in her voice. 'It looks like you got it second-hand from Moses.'

'I know! Look at the state of it.'

I didn't want to tell her that that was the only handset that Mum had been able to afford. My brain was working overtime as I thought of an excuse. I was getting good at lying.

'My good phone fell down the loo, so I had to have this old thing.'

I hoped she wouldn't see the blush that I could feel spreading across my cheeks. If she did see, she didn't comment.

'Well, we can't have that. First stop, the phone shop. Let's go get you something you can be proud of.'

I didn't know what to say. This scenario hadn't come up in my plan. I decided to just go with the flow and see what happened. Juju was already slipping on some gold ballerina pumps. It seemed that when she made a decision, nothing could hold her back. I had to run across the apartment to catch up with her, and then she was out of the door and pressing the lift button before I had time to think.

We stepped out of the front door and onto the street outside. It was busy. There were taxis and cars and a couple of bikes passing by, and I could still hear the children's voices. I hadn't really got my bearings, but it didn't matter, as Juju knew exactly where she was going. She walked really fast and I was almost jogging to keep up with her. Pretty soon we were walking down a big shopping street, and then we turned left, and there was Selfridges with its flags dangling in the non-existent breeze.

'I don't think they sell phones in there,' Juju said. 'But there's bound to be a phone shop round here somewhere, and then we'll go and get you some clothes, darling. Isn't this so much fun?'

Before I had chance to reply, Juju was dodging through the traffic and over the road. She saw a phone shop and darted into it. Once inside, she flitted from display to display, and then, unable to see exactly what she wanted, she just stood there in the middle of the shop and shouted, 'Please could somebody help me?' At which point, three men with 'Here to Help' written on their polo shirts in big red letters made a beeline for her from different corners of the shop. A handsome guy with a wide smile that showed his incredibly white teeth got to her first.

'Yes, madam. How can I help?'

I couldn't believe it. When Mum and I went shopping, we spent most of the time trying to avoid the shop assistants, and we certainly didn't summon them to our side.

'I'm wanting a new phone for my …' She paused and looked at me as she tried to decide how to describe me. I held my breath. 'My daughter,' she continued, and gave me an enormous wink.

I could feel myself swelling with pride that I was the daughter of this beautiful woman.

'We want the latest thing. No expense spared and a full contract with unlimited texts so we can keep in touch.'

'Certainly, madam. This is the latest handset. Obviously it has a touch screen and is capable of downloading all the latest apps, but it can also …'

I stopped listening after that. I couldn't concentrate on what he was saying. I was just totally overwhelmed by what was happening to me. Juju was asking questions and smiling at the phone man as if he was her best friend or something. It seemed to be working. He was desperate to please her – pathetic really. He produced various handsets, and Juju fiddled with them all, and then, almost as an afterthought, she turned to me.

'Well, Kitty. Which one do you like?'

I had no idea. I knew nothing about phones. There hardly seemed any point in following the latest handsets when there was no chance of me ever having one.

'I don't mind,' I managed. 'They are all fantastic. Which one do you think will be best?'

Juju looked at me and smiled. She seemed pleased that I was letting her make the decision, and I was glad that I'd pleased her, even if it was by accident.

'I think …' She was holding a phone in each hand and weighing them like a pair of scales. 'This one. We'll take this one. Is that OK with you, Kitty?'

I just nodded. Any of them would have been perfect.

'So, young man. Let's get through the paperwork as quickly as possible. We have a lot of shopping to do and we are on a tight time schedule. If you can't sort this out for us in ten minutes, then I'm afraid we may self-combust.'

The sales assistant looked as if he was taking her at her word and almost broke into a run to the desk at the back of the shop.

He started taking her through the paperwork, trying to explain the various packages that were available, but she cut him short.

'Don't give me all those tedious details. Which is the best?'

He was just answering her when she turned to me, cutting him off mid-sentence.

'Three hundred minutes with unlimited text and data suit you?'

I didn't know what to say. Not only was my phone fresh from the ark, but it was also on a pay-as-you-go tariff, and I was under strict instructions never to go over ten pounds a month. Juju decided to answer her own question, as I seemed to have lost the power of speech.

'Yes. That's the one. Now then, darling. Where do I sign?'

She put her manicured hand on the sales assistant's arm and gave a little squeeze. Five minutes later we left the shop, and I was the owner of a brand-new, state-of-the-art phone.

'Right,' said Juju. 'Selfridges next!'

It was fun, shopping with Juju. She didn't do it like Mum. Instead of going with a clear plan in mind, Juju just raced from one department to the next as the mood took her, her eye caught by something that would result in a massive change of direction. We started by looking at make-up. She got me to sit on one of those leather stools right in the middle of the Fragrance Hall, and then she waited until one of the make-up women came. As one approached us, her super-white tunic almost glowing, Juju smiled at her and waved her hand in the air. She didn't quite click her fingers but she might as well have done.

'My daughter is about to learn one of the most important lessons in a woman's life,' she began.

I held my breath, anxious to know what monumental event

was about to happen to me.

'How to apply make-up effectively.'

She smiled and the woman in white returned her smile knowingly. I felt as if I was about to be initiated into some secret society.

'An ability to control your make-up is what separates the cans from the cannots in this world,' she continued. 'You, Kitty darling, are most definitely going to be a can kind of woman.'

I was just twinkling inside, basking in her certainty in my future even though I wasn't entirely sure that I could live up to her expectations.

Then she said to the woman, 'Nothing too heavy. She's got plenty of time for all that. Just something to liven up her complexion and bring out those amazing eyes.'

The make-up woman nodded, as if this somewhat cryptic instruction was all she needed, and set to work. After twenty minutes she offered me a small round mirror, and I looked into it to gaze at the new me. I was a bit disappointed at first. I think I'd been expecting some miracle transformation, and when I looked in the mirror, it was just me looking back. But then I looked a bit more closely. My skin had taken on this kind of glow. I looked like me, just a lot healthier, and my eyes looked much larger, the grey really emphasised by a pale green shadow, and my lashes, already quite long, looked even longer and curled slightly, which made my eyes look bigger. A little bit of lip gloss finished the look. I was delighted.

'You look gorgeous, sweet pea,' Juju said, and lifted her hand to touch my cheek. I almost flinched, not wanting her to smudge my new make-up, but the gesture was so gentle that I felt myself moving my head towards her hand, a bit like Merlin does when I stroke his head.

'That's perfect. We'll take everything that you've used to achieve that look together with a set of brushes. Now, you need a make-up bag. I assume you haven't got one.'

I shook my head. I did have a make-up bag that had come with bath bombs one Christmas, but I didn't want to miss the chance of something else new.

'Where will we find them?' she asked the woman in white, who indicated across the floor to a stand. 'Perfect. You package those up for us and we'll just go and choose one. We'll be right back.'

If I'd said that to a shop assistant, they would probably have thought that it was just an excuse and I was about to do a runner, but Juju spoke with a kind of authority that shop assistants seemed to obey. It was amazing. The woman began selecting all the products from a drawer under the counter. I could happily have just stood there and watched her package my new things, but Juju grabbed me by the hand and we were off.

As we stood before the brightly coloured pouches of all shapes and sizes, she said, 'Now, a woman always needs two make-up bags. A big one to store most things in, and a small one to carry around what you might need for touching up when you go out. But I don't suppose you'll be going out much, especially as you're grounded …' She looked at me slyly. 'So let's choose a big one to be going on with. Which do you like?'

I stared at the enormous selection, not really knowing where to start. Juju was picking them off the stand one by one to examine their various pockets and zips, so I did the same. My eyes were drawn to a rectangular bag with tiny little daisies on the outside, and so I unhooked that one from the display. It had two compartments inside, and Juju nodded her head in approval.

'Good choice. Right, let's go and collect your bits and pieces.'

Grabbing the make-up bag from me, she strode back to the counter and handed it over to the woman in white to pack with the rest. I almost fainted when she told Juju how much it had all come to, but Juju didn't bat an eyelid and just handed over her gold credit card. I couldn't remember ever having so much money spent on me in one day.

'Right, clothes next?' she asked purposefully.

I must have looked doubtful, because then she added, 'No. Let's save that for another day. Let's go and find some coffee, and then you might have to think about heading home. What time do the auditions finish?'

She winked at me and I grinned back.

'Around five, so I had better be leaving around four, I suppose.'

I was disappointed to have to leave when I was having so much fun. Juju looked at her watch.

'Just time for a quick one, then. Come on!' and she grabbed my hand and we were off again, negotiating our way through the crowds to the food hall, where despite the huge number of people, Juju managed to grab us a table and had a waiter at our feet in a matter of moments. She ordered coffee for herself and lemonade and a chocolate brownie for me. She just looked at me as I ate.

'You know, sweet pea,' she said eventually. 'It's so lovely having you in my life. I've had a fabulous afternoon taking you out and buying you things. Wait till we go clothes shopping. That will be in-cred-i-ble!'

She emphasised each syllable as she spoke, and I smiled back at her, my mouth full of chocolate.

I realised then that I still had never talked to Juju about the original plan. I was supposed to be getting her to help Mum and yet I had never mentioned it to her. Somehow it never seemed the right time to bring it up. Now I was beginning to wonder if the arrangement worked better like this. Whilst I still hated lying to Mum, I was enjoying having two mothers, especially when they were both so different to one another. I decided there and then to leave things as they were.

On the train on the way home, I started looking at all my gifts. I wasn't sure how I was going to get it all in the house without Mum noticing. And there was another problem. I could hardly start using my new phone. Not only would Mum spot it at once, but it also had a different number to mine, so I couldn't even use it when Mum wasn't there. The only person that I could ever contact with it was Juju, but as I sat on the train and it raced me back to my other life, that didn't seem too awful.

Chapter 19

We rocked on like that for a while. I did some research on the school play. The real rehearsals were twice a week at lunchtime and once after school, but that didn't suit my purposes. Rehearsals during the school day got me nowhere, and there wasn't enough time to get to Juju's and back after school. So, as far as Mum was concerned, we rehearsed every Saturday afternoon. She never once questioned it, and as the weeks went on, I stopped feeling guilty.

I couldn't really use my new phone except for texting Juju. It had a different kind of SIM card to my old one, so I couldn't just swap them over. I wondered about giving my school friends the new number, but I would still have to carry the old one about with me so that I could get in touch with Mum. In the end, I kept the old one for texts and calls, and used the new one for games and music and things. I kept it hidden though. I didn't want people asking questions about where I'd got the money for such a flash phone.

The make-up caused me similar problems. I couldn't wear it at home. Eagle-eyed Mum could spot a hint of mascara at forty paces. I tried carrying bits of it around with me and putting some on when I got to school, but then I had the problem of getting it off again before I got home, and it all just got too complicated. I used to get it out and look at it though. When Mum thought I was doing my homework, I'd line up all the little pots and pallets in size order on my bed. The brushes felt so soft on my skin. Mum nearly caught me a couple of times, but I always managed to get it out of sight by throwing my duvet over it all before she saw and started asking questions.

One Saturday, I'd arranged to go to Juju's as normal. It was kind of our routine by then and I was enjoying it. Sometimes we went out for food, sometimes we went for a walk around the shops, although I tried not to let her buy me stuff, because it was so difficult to keep things secret from Mum. I arrived at the apartment and she buzzed me in. I found her in the lounge watching the news. I was surprised. She always seemed too dynamic to just sit and watch telly, but this wasn't an ordinary day, as I discovered.

She was lying sprawled across one of the massive sofas. She was still wearing her dressing gown but I was sort of used to this by now. There was a bottle of champagne open on the glass coffee table with a used glass by the side of it. Juju had a glass in her hand but it was almost empty. Her face was a bit puffy and it looked as if she might have been crying, but as she had no make-up on, it was hard to tell. This wasn't the Juju that I knew, and I felt put off balance by the whole scene.

When she heard the door open, she shouted over to me. Her voice was louder than it needed to be. It wasn't a small apartment, but it wasn't that far from the door to the sofa.

'Kitty darling. I'm soooo glad to see you. Come in. Sit down here, next to me.'

She struggled to sit up, and I realised that she must have had most of the champagne herself. Then, as I walked over to where she was, I noticed a second bottle on its side under

129

the sofa. I felt a bit uncomfortable. Last time I had been with anyone who was drunk, it had been Lydia, and look how that had turned out. And Juju was an adult. She was supposed to be looking after me, not the other way around. What if there was a fire or something?

Anyway, I ignored all that and went to sit over where she was as she'd asked me to do. She moved her legs out of the way and folded them into her body and then wrapped her arms around them so that she was like a little ball. She rested her cheek on her knees and looked at me.

'I'm so awfully glad that you came to find me, my little Kitty baby. You do know that, don't you?'

I nodded. I didn't really know what else to say. I started biting at the skin around my fingernails, wishing that I could have the other, normal Juju instead.

'Oh!' she said as if she'd suddenly remembered something. 'Where are my manners? Have some champagne, Kitty. Run to the kitchen and get yourself a glass. Or you could use this one.'

She eyed the dirty glass on the coffee table and then thought better of it.

'No. Maybe not. It will have his germs on it. Go get a fresh glass, darling, and then we can have a toast.'

I didn't really want any champagne. I'd had a sip once on Christmas Day with Mrs Marshall, and I didn't like it at all.

'I'll get some Coke,' I mumbled, and stood up again to go to the kitchen.

'Coke!' she said. 'Did someone mention coke. That would be just dandy.'

'Should I bring you a can?' I asked, hopeful to get her away from the remains of the champagne bottle.

'Oh. That kind of coke! No, thank you, darling. I'll stick with this, thank you.'

She started giggling, although I really couldn't see what was so funny. As I left, she was trying to pour another glass of champagne into the narrow neck of the glass, not altogether successfully.

I went through to the kitchen. When I opened the door I was surprised to see the remains of a takeaway curry out on the usually pristine work surface. I heard myself suck my breath in when I saw a splodge of orange curry sauce on the beautiful white surface. I grabbed a piece of kitchen roll from under the sink and wiped it away, but it left a pale orange stain. I was going to try and find some bleach or something to clear it up, but then Juju shouted for me from the lounge.

'Kitty darling. Where are you?'

Her voice whined like a kid as if I'd been gone for hours, when in fact it was probably less than a minute.

'I'm coming,' I shouted back, and then got myself a Coke from the bottom of the fridge and headed through to where she was curled up on the sofa.

I sat back down and opened the can gently so that it didn't explode all over the cream cushions.

'I'm afraid there's a stain on the worktop. I could try to get it off for you if you like. Have you got any bleach?'

She looked at me as if I was talking in Swahili, so I tried again.

'In the kitchen. The curry sauce has made a stain on the work surface.'

She batted my words away with her elegant hand.

'Oh, that. No, darling. Don't worry about it. The maid will sort it when she comes in. Nothing for you to worry your little head about. Now, tell me things. How is the show going?'

And then she burst into fits of giggles.

'Of course, there is no show. Silly me! That's our little secret, isn't it? Shhhhhh!'

She put her finger to her lips but she couldn't quite hit her mouth, and her words were all blurring into one another. I didn't like it at all. I was wondering whether I should make an excuse and just go home, when she stopped giggling and fell quiet.

'Have you ever wondered who your daddy is? Not your dead daddy. Your real daddy.'

She just came out with it, just like that, as if she was talking about what we were having for tea. I was so shocked that I didn't know what to say at first. I had wondered, of course, but I'd decided that finding one birth parent was enough for the time being.

'Well, sometimes,' I said slowly. 'I mean, it would be strange not to, wouldn't it?'

I didn't say anything else. I didn't know what to say. I was nervous about asking any questions in case she clammed up, and yet at the same time, I wasn't sure that I really wanted to know.

'He was here. Just now.'

What, here? In the apartment? I didn't know what to think. I wondered if he was still here, and I looked around even though I was pretty certain that we were on our own. Then my eyes settled on the second champagne glass. She saw me taking it in and she must have followed my thought pattern.

'No. Not him,' she said with a nod to the glass too. 'He's a rat, and you must never have anything to do with rats, Kitty. They're dirty and nasty.'

I wasn't really sure I was following what was going on. Had

132

she had two men in her apartment at the same time? Was one of them my birth father? Was that why she'd been crying? I was completely lost. She must have seen it on my face.

'Not here, silly!'

She giggled again and knocked back the glass of champagne, pulling a face afterwards as if it wasn't that nice a thing to have done.

'No. I haven't seen your dad … your real dad, I mean … not your dead dad. I haven't seen him to speak to since 1998. Well, I mean, I see him nearly every day, but he never sees me.'

I was completely lost. I didn't like her talking like that and I couldn't understand all her riddles. She seemed to be getting drunker by the minute, and I knew I should just leave and go home, but I couldn't seem to move. Now that she had spoken about my birth father, I needed to know everything.

She was waving her empty champagne glass in the direction of the TV.

'In there. On there. Whatever. That's where I see him. He's on there.'

She dissolved into giggles again, leaving me in total confusion.

'Hang on!' I finally found my voice. 'Are you saying that my father …?' I corrected myself. 'My birth father is on the telly?'

'Got it in one. Have a banana! What a clever girl you are? He was just here a moment ago. Wait! Let me find him.'

She lurched towards the coffee table and picked up the remote. The news had finished now and they were doing the weather forecast. She pressed the rewind button, and the last few minutes began flying past backwards, and then suddenly she stopped, and there on the screen was a man. He was standing on the grass outside the Houses of Parliament, talking to the camera. He was wearing a dark suit with a pale pink shirt and no tie. He had dark hair brushed back from his forehead and he had little round glasses on, a bit like Harry Potter. He looked alright. Nothing special. Nice enough but you wouldn't turn to look at him in the street. Except for the fact that he was famous – well, not famous exactly, but he was on the news most nights. I'd seen him plenty of times before.

'There you are!' said Juju.

Her voice sounded cold and bitter somehow, not a bit like it usually was.

'Sam Cunningham. Daddy dearest.'

She leant forward to pour herself another glass, but only a dribble came out. She bounced the bottle up and down a bit as if that would help and then tossed it aside. I watched in horror as the heavy green bottle flew through the air, but it landed without doing any damage on the sofa opposite.

Honestly, I did not know what to do. My head was full of questions, but Juju didn't look as if she was capable of answering any of them. How could this man, Sam Cunningham, who was in our lounge every night, standing in front of some building or other and talking about the Prime Minister, possibly be my birth father? I looked at him as he did his piece to camera, searching his face for any clue, any suggestion that we might possibly be related, but I couldn't see anything.

'Him?' I asked eventually. 'Sam Cunningham? The reporter guy? He's my dad? Are you sure?'

This last bit just came out. I didn't mean to imply that Juju didn't know who my dad might be. It was just that it was so difficult to take it all in out of the blue like that. Fortunately, she didn't seem to have taken offence.

'Yes, darling. Him. Sam "Look at me! Haven't I done well

for myself?" Cunningham. We were at school together. Did you not know? No. Of course you didn't. Silly me. He was my childhood sweetheart. Picked me up and used me, broke my heart and then ran for the hills. I never saw him again until he got his big break at the BBC. Now I see him all the time. He is your father. Sorry about that, sweet pea.'

Even though her eyes didn't seem to be focusing very well, they looked so sad, and I thought for a moment she was going to cry again. I didn't know what to say. I didn't even know what to think. His piece to camera had finished and it had gone back to the studio. I grabbed the remote from Juju and rewound it again. Could it be true? As I watched him, he seemed to be talking to me alone, staring down the lens of the camera at me, his daughter. And if what Juju said was right and he had done a runner, then he didn't know anything about me, didn't know that I even existed.

I had so many questions but Juju had closed her eyes, and I could tell from her breathing that she had fallen asleep. I rewound the news item one last time, searching for a clue, anything, but still I could see nothing in Sam Cunningham's face that might link him to me.

I turned to look at Juju surrounded by the empty bottles. Then I stood up and walked to the front door, closing it gently behind me.

I don't know how I found my way back home. I just kept thinking of Sam Cunningham and his dark hair and his Harry Potter glasses. Sam Cunningham – my father.

Chapter 20

It didn't occur to me as I arrived home that I was probably at least an hour earlier than expected, so when Mum asked me why I was back so soon, I must have looked really confused. After a couple of moments, I managed to mumble something about rehearsal being shorter than usual and went straight to my room. Mum called out after me to see if I was OK. She can always tell when something is wrong. I just shouted back that I was fine but that I had homework to do.

Once in my room with the door shut, I got Juju's phone out of my bag and found Google. Then I typed in 'Sam Cunningham'. Immediately images of my father filled the screen. The first entry was a BBC one, then Wikipedia, then more entries all the way down to the bottom of the page. I clicked on Wikipedia, clicking my nails impatiently as I waited for the page to load. It was difficult to read on such a small screen but there he was.

Samuel Robert Cunningham. Born on 15 September 1982 in Guildford, Cunningham went to Bristol University, where he read history and politics. He began his career as a journalist for the BBC and then switched to working in front of the camera ...

There were lots of other details, but the facts swam in front of my eyes. I gave up trying to read them and just clicked on one of the images to bring it up large. I stared at it. Could I see any part of myself staring back? Something around the mouth maybe? I couldn't tell.

There were so many questions flying round my head. When were he and Juju together? Did he know that he had a baby? Did he have a family of his own? But I had no way of answering them. I assumed that Juju would still be asleep, so there was no point ringing her, and anyway, Mum would wonder who I was talking to. I would just have to wait.

I wished I hadn't fallen out with Lydia, or rather she hadn't fallen out with me. Normally, I would have texted her and she would have raced round to help. As it was, I had no one to talk to. The only person left was Juju, and she had let me down. I surprised myself when this thought came into my head. It was the first time that anything negative about her had crossed my mind. It was true though. She had let me down. She'd been expecting me and yet she was drunk when I arrived, as if she didn't care whether I was there or not. Then she'd been so brutal about Dad. I knew enough about it to know that that was probably just the booze talking, but even so, it still hurt.

Well, it didn't really matter who my birth father was. I wasn't interested. I had enough parents already, especially as one of them didn't know about the other. This whole thing was already too complicated without making it any worse. I looked again at the photograph of Sam Cunningham on my phone. If I screwed my eyes up and squinted at it, I thought I could see a hint of my top lip and maybe my nose. The family resemblance wasn't massively obvious like it was when I looked at Juju, but it was there in the background, if I really peered hard.

I closed the page down and lay back on my bed to think.

They must have been seventeen or eighteen when Juju got pregnant. Still at school and in the sixth form. Sam had gone on to university, so it didn't seem to have made any difference to his life. He must have done the deed and then abandoned her to deal with the consequences by herself. I knew from something that she'd said that Juju never went to university. She had made some joke about learning at the University of Life, but she had sounded bitter when she spoke, like it wasn't really funny. Having me must have messed up her A levels and with them her chances. No such problems for Sam, it seemed. He must have dumped her and run for the hills.

And this man was my father? Well, I certainly didn't want anything to do with him. I had had a dad and he was the best dad a girl could wish for. Sam Cunningham, with his floppy hair and his stupid glasses, was nothing to do with me.

I kind of wished that Juju hadn't told me. I don't suppose she meant to. It was just an unfortunate coincidence – her having the champagne and the TV being on and Sam being on it. It must have been harder for her though. She had known for all those years, even before I got in touch, that Sam was my father. He'd been in her lounge, in my lounge, every day for years. There was no way that she could escape from him. He was just there, on her TV.

I picked the Juju phone up to text her. I even started to type, but then I changed my mind. I wasn't sure what I wanted to say. Perhaps it would be better if I waited to see what she said to me first. No doubt she'd wake up a bit later on, remember what happened and text to see if I was OK. What if she didn't remember? What if I had to remind her of the whole horrible afternoon?

It was all going round and round in my head. I needed

138

something to distract me. I put the phone back in my bag where Mum wouldn't see it and then went to the lounge. I thought about watching some TV, but there was always the chance that Sam Cunningham would pop up, so instead, I got out a DVD and put it in the machine.

'Mum,' I called, 'I'm going to watch *Mamma Mia*. Do you fancy watching it with me? We can put the singalong words on if you like.'

Mum emerged from the kitchen almost at once.

'What a good idea,' she said. 'I was just going to start on the ironing, but do you know what? It can jolly well wait till tomorrow. Budge up.'

She dropped onto the sofa just where I was sitting, and I squealed and shuffled along a bit. As the film started and Mum and I wriggled into comfortable positions, I wondered why I had ever thought it was a good idea to go off in search of Juju in the first place.

Chapter 21

Life ticked on around me and I tried to work out what I thought of it all. It wasn't easy. Juju had let me down and thrown a hand grenade into the mix while she was at it. She sent me a text the next day saying that she was sorry, although I noticed that she didn't say precisely what she was sorry for, and I wondered if she could even remember what had happened. I sent her one back saying that it didn't matter – but it did.

I watched the news religiously. Although Sam Cunningham wasn't on every time, when he did appear, I got such a buzz because I knew something that he didn't. When he was moving, rather than just being frozen in a photo, I could see more of my face in his. It felt so weird, after not looking like anyone for my whole life, to suddenly have two relations, and I loved to just stare at him. One evening, Mum was watching with me when he came onto the screen. I took a sly look at her to see if she reacted to him, but there was nothing there that I could see.

'I'm glad you're starting to take an interest in the world about you, Kitty,' she said, smiling and nodding proudly. I felt the now familiar pang of guilt stab me in the heart. 'It's important to look further than the end of your street if you want to make the most of your life.'

Of course, I couldn't tell her that I still found the news as terminally boring as I always had done and that it was something else that had caught my interest. Like my birth father.

On top of the Sam Cunningham stuff, there was another major development in my life. A bit of a thawing between me and Lydia. Well, I say 'thaw'. That's something of an exaggeration. The very tip of the enormous iceberg that she had grown between us melted just a bit.

At break time, I noticed that there was a big hoo-ha going on around Lydia. This was nothing new. Even before we fell out, Lydia had a tendency towards high drama. If there was ever the opportunity to bring a sense of the theatre to a situation, then Lydia would find it. She should have been in the school play, not me. (Not that I was, of course!) Anyway, I was pretending not to be interested in whatever crisis was unfolding around Lydia, but of course I was. Not much happens at school, so all diversions are welcome. As far as I could gather, Lydia had lost some money. It sounded as if she'd dropped her purse on the way to school or left it at home or something. Losing the purse wasn't the problem though. The problem was that she hadn't got any money and so she couldn't get any lunch. After huge amounts of arm-waving and bag-emptying, it was finally established that her purse was not there.

'What am I going to do?' she was wailing. 'I'm starving already and it's double PE this afternoon. There is no way that I can run about on that hockey pitch for two hours if I haven't had any lunch.'

She opened her big eyes and flicked her blonde hair and looked at her new friends. This should be interesting, I thought. Lydia had clearly hoped that the spelling out of her predicament would be enough for her friends to all rush to her, open-pursed to help their leader out of her financial embarrassment. But nobody did. First they stared at Lydia, and then, when they realised that she was expecting them to lend her some cash, they all stared at their shoes. Not one of them offered her a bean. No one even suggested that she might like to share their lunch. It was interesting to watch Lydia's face as it changed from an image of expectation to shock that not only were her so-called friends going to let her starve rather than share with her, but she really wasn't going to be able to get herself some food.

I can't say I was enjoying her misfortune. Lydia had been my best friend for a long time and you can't just turn that off overnight. I did feel a bit sorry for her, but what was really interesting was seeing how flaky her new friends were. They didn't even make excuses as to why they couldn't help. They just stood there for a bit, looking uncomfortable, and then shuffled off, pretending to be interested in something that was going on near the tennis courts. Lydia was left all by herself.

I didn't really think about what I did next. If I had done, then I might not have said anything for fear of the tongue-lashing that I could have got from her. I stood where I was, and in as clear a voice as I could manage, I said, 'I've got some money. I could lend you some if you like.'

She looked round to see where the voice was coming from. I don't think that she had noticed that I was even there. When she saw it was me, she looked a bit shocked.

'I've got an emergency fiver,' I said, 'that Mum gave me ... well ... for emergencies. You can borrow it if it'd help.'

Her eyes narrowed, and I could see that she was trying to work out whether this was some kind of trick, whether

I was going to offer the cash and then when she accepted, withdraw the offer and humiliate her still further. I just raised my eyebrows. She knew me, what I was like. I wasn't about to make it easy for her – she had been too nasty to me over the past few weeks for that – but I wasn't going to make her grovel either. All she had to do was ask.

We stood like that in silence for what seemed like ages. The others had made their escape complete by wandering over to watch the scrap that had broken out between some Year 9 boys. Just when I thought she either hadn't heard me or couldn't bring herself to take my money, she said, 'Well, if you don't mind, that would be great.'

She pulled her mouth into a twist that might have been a smile, although it was hard to be sure.

'I don't mind at all,' I said, enjoying the moral high ground. 'I'll need it back though. In case there's another emergency!'

I smiled at her, a full, proper one to show that even though she had been a complete cow to me and I would be entirely within my rights to chop her head off and feed it to the worms, I was a nicer person than that. I started digging round in my bag. The money was in a beaten-up brown envelope in one of the pockets. Exercise books and my ruler and calculator and all sorts were threatening to spill out all over the floor as I riffled through, so I rested my bag on a bench so that I could have a better look. As I delved right down to the bottom, Lydia caught a glimpse of Juju's phone.

'Got a new phone? Looks like a good one. Bit of a change to the old Batphone.'

She didn't say it in a particularly jokey way, but I'd known her long enough to understand that this was a nod to humour. We'd often laughed at the old-fashioned phone that I'd been saddled with. And in that moment, I forgot that this was Lydia, who had unfairly disowned me and, by force of habit alone, I became conspiratorial.

'I know! It's ace, isn't it? Juju bought it for me.'

As soon as the words were out of my mouth, I regretted it. I didn't know whether I could trust Lydia any more, and she certainly didn't deserve to get any top gossip.

She looked at me, forehead creased, as if she was expecting me to say more, but at that moment, I finally found the dog-eared envelope with the emergency fiver in it and handed it over.

'Here you are,' I said. 'You can give it back to me tomorrow.'

Then I picked up my bag and walked away. I heard her shout, 'Thanks,' but I didn't turn round. I didn't want her to see my face. I was grinning from ear to ear. So much for her new mates, the Bell twins and all the others. Where were they when the chips were down? Nowhere, that's where. No, it was me, reliable old Kitty, who had dug Lydia out of a hole, who had looked beyond all the really nasty things she had said to me about stuff that really wasn't my fault and done her a good deed. It felt great.

I wasn't sure whether it would lead to anything. Sometimes I'd thought that I wouldn't have her back as my best friend if she came crawling on hands and knees, but if I was really honest, I did miss her. I had other friends, of course. It wasn't as if I was on my own, but it wasn't the same as having a best friend who you could have a laugh with and tell everything to, and let's face it, I had plenty to tell. But I wasn't ready for that yet. Lydia had hurt me, really hurt me, and she was going to have to spend quite a bit of time rebuilding my trust if we were going to get anywhere near where we were before. This might be a start though.

The next day, she came to find me at break. I was glad to see that she'd come on her own, not with her entourage in tow.

'I brought you this,' she said, offering me a handful of change that together might add up to five pounds.

It wasn't really the same as a handy five-pound note that I could hide in my bag, but at least she had thought about it and brought it for me.

'Thanks,' she said again. 'You got me out of a hole.'

She held my gaze, and if I'd wanted to, I could have read something into her look, but it was too early for that, so I just smiled back and said thank you. Then I walked away.

Chapter 22

Mum never snoops around in my room. It's not something she's ever done. When I listen to other girls talking about their mums trying to hack their Facebook accounts or read their text messages, I always smile smugly and say, 'My mum's not like that. She trusts me.' I don't think she was snooping this time either. She was trying to find something, although we never established precisely what. Anyway, she went in my wardrobe and found the make-up bag and all the brushes and things. When I got home, everything that Juju had bought me was laid out in a long line on the table in the lounge together with all the brushes in their black leather roll. When I saw them all sitting there like that, I knew there was going to be trouble. They just reeked of expensive.

I always think that you can tell if something is wrong the moment you walk in somewhere. The bad thing hangs about in the atmosphere and spoils it, like a smell ... or a ghost. Anyway, I'd been to the minimart to get an onion for Mum, and I'd only been gone a few minutes. When I got back, I headed for the kitchen, but Mum shouted for me before I could get there.

'Kitty. Could you come in here, please?'

Mum's voice sounded serious, and at first I thought that there must have been an accident or something, but as soon as

I opened the lounge door and saw the row of make-up on the table, I knew exactly what was wrong.

'Kitty. I was in your wardrobe looking for … well … looking for something, and I came across this little lot.'

She looked at me expectantly, waiting for an explanation.

My mind went into overdrive. I thought about exploding into outraged indignation that she had been going through my stuff, but I could see that all that would do was put off the inevitable. I was still going to have to explain why I had over two hundred pounds' worth of expensive make-up hidden in my bedroom. What I really needed was time to think through the ramifications of all the excuses that I could give. Unfortunately, time was not on my side. Mum was staring at me and I could see her patience evaporating before my eyes.

'It's Lydia's,' I said quickly.

It was the first thing that popped into my head.

'What do you mean, it's Lydia's? I thought you and Lydia had fallen out.'

'Well, we have. Well, we had. It's getting a bit better actually. I lent her my emergency fiver because she didn't have any money for lunch, and her so-called friends wouldn't let her borrow any. It's OK, though, because she paid me back.'

'Well, why is it all hidden here, in your wardrobe?'

'It wasn't hidden.'

'Well, it was hardly sitting at the top,' Mum said abruptly.

It was true. The make-up had been buried at the bottom of the wardrobe under a shoebox. If Mum had found it, then she must have been looking for something pretty hard. I thought I saw Mum blush, just a bit. I didn't speak as I tried to work out what she'd been after.

'Well?' she said, cutting across my thoughts. 'Why have you

got at least a hundred pounds' worth of make-up supposedly belonging to Lydia hidden in your wardrobe?'

At least she didn't have any idea just how expensive it had been.

'It's been here for ages,' I said.

I could feel the start of a feasible story beginning to form in my head. I continued slowly, allowing it to grow as it came out.

'She left it here before we went to Kyle's party. And then, when we fell out, I didn't feel like giving it back to her and she didn't ask for it, so I just left it there.'

'Is that the party that you went to without my knowledge or permission? The one where Lydia behaved like an idiot, putting you and her in danger? The one that her mother was happy to leave you at until God knows what time in the morning?'

I could tell that Mum was enjoying her rant. I hadn't realised she was still so angry about the party, but this level of anger gave me an idea of the kind of ear-burning she must have given to Lydia's mum. And that would explain why Lydia was so very annoyed with me. Not that that was an excuse.

I nodded in what I hoped was a very sorry kind of way.

'Yes, Mum. That party. Anyway, we were here practising our make-up before we went—'

'Stop!' interrupted Mum. 'I don't want to hear any more. It's bad enough knowing that you went to the party without telling me, but hearing that you had planned the whole thing out long enough in advance to be practising your make-up makes me feel sick to my stomach. Well, you can take this little lot –' she swept everything into one pile and began stuffing it into the bag '– and give it back to that little madam Lydia. You are both far too young for make-up like this. It's a designer brand. It must have cost a fortune. Cheryl clearly has more money than sense if she's spending that kind of money on a twelve-year-old. I've a good mind to throw the whole lot in the bin. Lydia clearly doesn't appreciate it. I mean, how long has it been here? Weeks! Life's not all about money, you know?'

This comment wasn't really directed at me. Sometimes Mum just went off on one. Something would set her off and then she'd rant for ages. It was always obvious that she wasn't moaning about the thing that had started it but something else. The trouble was I was never quite sure what the something else was. Anyway, I'd learned that it was best just to nod, keep my mouth shut and wait until she'd finished.

'In fact, I've got a good mind to take this little lot round to Lydia's myself and tell that mother of hers exactly what I think of her ludicrous spending habits.'

Uh-oh. This was dangerous territory. Not only would this make things worse between me and Lydia just as we were starting to salvage something from our car crash of a friendship, but also Lydia would deny all knowledge of the make-up, and then I would have to tell Mum where I'd really got it from. I leant forward and took the make-up bag out of her hands. Apart from anything else, she was getting so worked up that she might just throw it and smash all my beautiful little pallets.

'It's OK, Mum. You don't need to do that,' I said as gently as I could. It was a bit like handling a toddler. 'I'll take it to school tomorrow and give it back then. Shall I make you a cup of tea?'

It sounded a bit feeble even to me. I looked at her, waiting for her to respond, and then I realised that I still had the onion in my hand.

'Oh, and I got your onion.'

I offered it up to her as if it were the most valuable gift in the world. Mum gave a half smile, but I could see that the rant hadn't really left her, and if I wasn't careful, I was going to catch it all over again, so I took the make-up bag and scarpered. I was going to have to find somewhere else to hide it, which was really tricky. I thought I could guarantee that Mum wouldn't look in my room, but it seemed I was wrong. Maybe she'd finished her nosing and I would be safe just putting it back where she'd found it. The whole thing was just really odd. I left it out on my bed. There was no need to hide it now when she thought I was taking it back to Lydia. I would come up with somewhere else to put it later on.

I made Mum her cup of tea, and then we cooked the bolognese sauce together and she seemed to forget all about her outburst. Later on, however, after I'd gone to bed, I heard her in the lounge. She was crying. Quietly. So I wouldn't hear. I lay in bed for a moment wondering what to do, then I got up and tiptoed down the corridor to the lounge. The door was open. Mum was sitting on the sofa with the coffee table pulled up next to her. On it was half a glass of red wine and a box of Asda value tissues. Then next to that I saw something that made my heart beat a little faster. It was the black box file, the one that Mum kept all our important papers in, the one where I had found Juju's name. The box was shut but Mum must have been looking through it. Otherwise, why else would it be there?

Mum reached for a tissue and gave her nose a long, shuddering blow. It sounded so ridiculous that it was all I could do not to giggle, but something told me that Mum wouldn't want me to see her so upset, so I backed down the corridor as quietly as I could and got back into bed before she could see me. Mum's muffled sobs were the last thing I heard before I fell asleep.

Chapter 23

Saturday came round and it was time for my 'rehearsal' again. I'd arranged to visit Juju as usual, but this time, rather than feeling excited about the trip, I was a bit anxious. Juju's gloss had tarnished a bit after the last trip, and having turned up when she was drunk and morose once, there was always the chance that it might happen again. That was definitely an experience that I didn't want to repeat. I had enough on with Mum bursting into tears for no obvious reason without Juju starting as well. I tossed the pros and cons around in my head for a bit, but in the end, I decided to give Juju a second chance. After all, it had only been the once and she was my birth mother.

I knew as soon as I stepped out of the lift that I'd made the right decision. Juju was at the open door waiting to greet me, and she was fully clothed in a tight pencil skirt and a short-sleeved blouse.

'Hi, darling,' she said, and stepped forward to give me a huge hug.

There hadn't been much hugging between us up until now, so it felt slightly awkward, but I took her enthusiasm to be a sign of how sorry she was, and let her squeeze me. She smelled expensive and clean.

'How are you? How's school? What's happening with Lydia?

Is she still being a little cow? Come in and tell me all. I want to know absolutely everything.'

She led the way into the lounge and I saw that she had made an effort there too. On the enormous glass coffee table was laid out the makings of a fantastic carpet picnic. There were little sandwiches, all neatly cut into triangles, and baby sausage rolls and four different kinds of crisps. There was also some carrot and celery sticks, which were less appealing, but which adults always seem to think are necessary at a picnic. In the middle sat a tray of tiny little cakes, all different, and some chocolate buttons in a glass dish. Next to the food were two white plates with pink serviettes on them and a couple of glasses. Juju started to split a can of Coke between us, waiting between each pour for the bubbles to settle.

'I've made us a little picnic to eat while we chat.' She looked at me a bit sheepishly and then added, 'I say "made", but really "bought" would be more accurate. You know me and cooking, darling.'

I wanted to point out that making sandwiches didn't really constitute cooking, but I didn't want to hurt her feelings or sound ungrateful, so I just said thank you and told her that I was starving. This wasn't true, as I'd bought a huge sausage roll to eat on the train, but I didn't think I'd have a problem eating a bit of something. It all looked delicious.

Then I told her about the week's developments. I told her about Lydia and the lunch money and how it felt like she might want to be my friend again.

Juju nodded as I spoke, and then said, 'Well, you be careful, sweet pea. People who blow hot and cold like that don't make the best friends. You need someone who'll stick with you no matter what happens.'

She narrowed her eyes as she spoke, and something about her voice made me think that she meant more than she said, but I didn't really understand what she was getting at.

I told her that I was being cautious with Lydia. She had hurt me really badly and you can't just bounce back from something like that, but I did prefer my life with Lydia in it rather than out of it. Then I told her about Mum finding all the make-up that she'd bought me.

Juju looked confused. 'Well, why did you have to hide it in the first place, darling? I didn't expect you to keep it under wraps.'

'Mum doesn't really like me wearing make-up,' I explained. 'She thinks I'm too young.'

Juju raised an eyebrow but she didn't say anything.

'And also I was worried that she'd think I'd nicked it or something. You can't buy that kind of stuff on the amount of pocket money that I have.'

'Fair point,' she said, nodding wisely. 'So what did you say?'

'I told Mum that it was Lydia's and that I hadn't given it back, because we'd fallen out and I was cross with her.'

'Cunning!' said Juju, and she winked at me mischievously.

'Well, not that cunning as it turned out, because that just made Mum cross again. She kept going on about how irresponsible it was of Lydia's mum to buy her such expensive make-up.'

As soon as the words were out of my mouth, I heard the implied criticism of Juju that was contained within them, but I couldn't do anything about it.

'Not that you're irresponsible or anything,' I added quickly in a futile attempt to undo the damage, but Juju didn't seem to have noticed.

153

'And that was about it for this week,' I said as I struggled to keep the blush that was creeping over my face under control.

I bit into another sandwich quick so that I didn't have to say anything else. I didn't mention about Mum having the black box file out or all the crying I had heard.

'Well, it's all go in your world, isn't it?' Juju said cheerfully, completely ignoring that I'd just sort of told her that she was an irresponsible mother.

We were quiet for a minute as we ate the food, Juju making little pleasured noises as she bit into something that appealed and turning her nose up at other stuff. When I'd eaten as many sandwiches and crisps as I could manage, I took a slurp of Coke and sat back into the sofa for a little break before I tackled the cakes.

'How about you? What have you been up to this week? Working hard?'

I don't know what made me ask. It was more something to say than anything else, and after all, why shouldn't I ask about her work? But Juju looked a bit cross, like I spoiled something by mentioning it. She didn't say anything for a moment, taking tiny bites of a prawn sandwich when she could just have easily popped the whole thing into her mouth at once.

'Work's fine, darling,' she said eventually. 'You know how it is. One week looks pretty much like another. I'm just glad when Saturday comes round and I get to spend some time with you.'

And that was it. She wasn't giving anything away, and I certainly didn't feel like I could ask again, so I circled my finger over the cake plate and chose a tiny chocolate éclair.

'Actually,' she said, 'there was something that I wanted to talk to you about, sweet pea.'

She was speaking a bit more quickly than usual. Here it comes, I thought.

'You know all that stuff that I said last week …?'

She paused, perhaps hoping that I would interrupt and fill the gaps, but I wasn't going to make it that easy for her, so I just looked at her expectantly. She tried again.

'Last Saturday, when you were here and I was a bit … emotional.'

Drunk, I thought, but again I held my tongue.

'Do you remember what I said about that bloke who was on the telly?'

I could pretend that I had forgotten about the whole sordid incident, but I had far too many questions to do that, so I played along.

'You mean when you told me that Sam Cunningham was my birth father?'

I wasn't taking any prisoners here, and apart from anything else, it was fun, having the upper hand for once. Juju looked even more uncomfortable than she had done before.

'Yes. I remember that,' I added. 'What about it?'

'Well, that was it really. I just wanted to know if you remembered, that was all.'

She wasn't getting away with it as lightly as that. I saw my chance and I went for it.

'Actually,' I said with my most angelic smile, 'I had some questions about that.'

'Oh?' she asked uncertainly.

'Yes. From what I can work out, Sam Cunningham, my birth father, must have been eighteen when I was born.'

She looked surprised.

'Lord! You have been doing your homework, haven't you?'

I ignored the question and ploughed on.

'So I reckon that you must have been at school when you were pregnant with me. Is that right?'

Juju seemed to relax a little, as if she was resigned to answering my questions now that I'd started asking them.

'Yes,' she said. 'That's right. We were at school together in Guildford. That's where I'm from, originally. Sam asked me out when I was fifteen.'

'When you were in Year 11?' I interrupted, and then wished I hadn't. I needed her to tell me all of this before she changed her mind and clammed up.

She thought about it for a moment.

'Yes, I suppose it must have been. He asked me at a party just before Christmas. He was already sixteen and I was almost. He was lovely. Tall and handsome. He didn't wear glasses then but he had the same kind of dark floppy hair. I was the envy of the school. Everybody wanted to go out with Sam Cunningham. And then we stayed together right though the sixth form. We were busy applying to universities when I found out that I was pregnant. Sam wanted to go to Bristol to study history and politics. He wanted to be a journalist even then. Always had his head in some newspaper or other. And I was going to apply to Bath to study ...'

Her voice kind of drifted off. I waited.

'We had it all planned. Not the same university but near enough to each other that we would be able to see each other at weekends. Only that's not how it worked out.'

Juju's face changed. She had looked quite dreamy when she was talking about the romance, but then her forehead creased and her voice became harsher.

'I found out that I was pregnant just as we sent our applications off. It was absolutely awful. I didn't know what to do. By the time I'd worked out what was happening, I was about four months gone. Did you know that by that stage, the baby is fully formed and about five inches long? It can suck its thumb and everything. I didn't know that either, but I found a book in the library and it told me. When I read that I knew I couldn't have an abortion.'

The information was coming at me too fast. I wanted her to slow down so I could fully absorb what she was saying, but at the same time, I was scared that if I interrupted her, she would stop talking, so I just sat still and tried to listen as hard as I could.

'Anyway, I told Sam one night after school. He'd come round to our house and we were in my bedroom. He was lying on my bed playing with a tennis ball and I was sitting at my desk. I could see a bump by that stage but I don't think anyone else had noticed it. I remember it like it was yesterday. He was talking about Bristol. We hadn't had our offers through at that point but he was pretty confident he'd get one. He was really clever, and the teachers at school had predicted high grades for him. And I said, I remember it so clearly, I said, "Well, I'm not sure I'll be able to go." He told me not to be so stupid. He thought I was just having doubts about getting the grades, and then I told him that I was pregnant. He asked if I was sure, which, of course, I was, and then he didn't say anything for the longest time. Then finally he said, "What are you going to do about it?" Not what are *we* going to do? What are *you* going to do? It was clear from the very beginning that he saw it as entirely my problem.'

That was me, I thought. A tiny baby, me. I was the problem. I tried to put myself in Juju's shoes but it was too difficult to imagine. I rearranged my face into what I hoped was a sympathetic expression, but by that stage, Juju wasn't really talking to me at all. She was retelling the story to herself, testing it in her memory. It was as if she was looking for the painful parts so that she could press them gently, like a bruise, to see how much they hurt.

'And that was that,' she continued. 'I screamed at him to get out. He left and I never spoke to him again. It was a bit difficult to start with, being in classes together, but it wasn't long before I had to tell my parents. They pulled me out of school so that I could go to this dreadful place for teenage mothers. That's where I had you, and then as soon as you were born, they took you away and I never saw you again.'

Tears were streaming down her face, and I shuffled across the sofa to put my arms around her.

'But I'm here now,' I whispered.

I really didn't know what else to say. I wasn't ready for all this emotion. It wasn't what I'd had in mind when I asked the question.

Juju seemed to compose herself. She wiped the tears away roughly with the back of her hand and continued.

'I never saw him again either – Sam, I mean. He got his grades and went off to Bristol. Of course, I failed my A levels, so Bath was totally out of the question. Not that it mattered. I wouldn't have wanted to be within a hundred miles of him.'

She spat the words out. I could see how much she hated him, and in that moment, I hated him too.

'Then one day he popped up on my TV. I nearly had a heart attack. That man who had ruined my life, in the corner of my drawing room.'

I didn't like to think of myself as being something that ruined her life, but I could see that she didn't really mean it like that, and anyway, it was hardly my fault. I didn't ask to be born.

'And that's it. The whole sorry tale. I assumed that I had to forget about you until you were grown up, and then perhaps you'd come looking for me. It never crossed my mind that you'd find me when you were only twelve. You are one resourceful young lady.'

She patted my knee and gave it a squeeze.

'So there you have it,' she said again. 'The story of me and Sam Cunningham in a nutshell.'

There were so many other gaps that needed filling in about what had happened to her after I had been adopted. She would have been eighteen by then and an adult. I wanted to know where she'd lived, what she'd done for money, whether her parents, my grandparents, had been there for her, or whether she'd been left to cope on her own. I needed to know it all, but there was something about her body language, the way she was staring into space, that made me understand that this was not the time for these questions. Juju had shared enough with me for the time being.

I moved closer to where she was sitting. She seemed smaller somehow than she had before, more vulnerable, and in that moment, I felt like it was me who was the one in control, the adult. I put my arms around her and she leant into me. I felt her body shake, and as she cried, I rubbed my hand up and down her back like Mum does to me when I'm upset.

'There, there,' I murmured.

I didn't know what else to say.

Chapter 24

It was hard trying to get my head around all the stuff that Juju had told me. The more I thought about it, the more sorry for her I felt. I couldn't believe that Sam, who had seemed like the perfect boyfriend, could desert her just when she'd needed him most. When I thought about the plans they'd made together and how he'd treated her when he found out about the baby, me, I wanted to scream. He had come out of it completely unscathed, his life totally unaffected by the minor inconvenience that was me. He had taken his A levels as planned and presumably done really well if he had been able to go to Bristol University. Meanwhile, Juju's life had fallen apart, all her dreams shattered. One mistake. One that they had both been equally responsible for, and yet she had taken all the flak. It was so unfair.

I didn't know Sam Cunningham from Adam, so it felt kind of wrong to be so angry with him, but I couldn't help it. I was so angry that I could spit. I needed someone to reassure me that I didn't have to love him just because he had been part of my creation, and I was desperate to talk to someone about it all. But who?

I couldn't talk to Juju. It was difficult enough for her and I didn't want to make things any worse. Mum was out too. I had travelled such a long way down this road without her. I couldn't just skip to the part about Sam Cunningham. I would need to explain the rest of it, and then we'd get lost in the fallout long before we got anywhere near this part of it.

I sometimes talked to Mrs Marshall about things when I couldn't talk to Mum. I thought about this possibility for quite a long time. I liked being in the chaos of her flat. I liked sitting and stroking Merlin as I told her stuff. It meant that I didn't have to look at her, because I was looking at the cat, and somehow that made it easier to talk. And there were the yummy cakes to consider. Then again, if I told Mrs Marshall, I felt pretty certain that she would feel the need to tell Mum, and if she was going to do that, then I might as well just tell Mum myself.

That left one person –Lydia.

Things between us had been slowly improving since the emergency fiver thing. She had stopped laughing at me if I approached her and her gang. In fact, her gang seemed to have dwindled quite a lot so that it was just her and the Bell twins most of the time. I'd seen her looking at me a bit, but then when she saw that I'd noticed, she'd turn away really quickly and pretend that she was doing something else.

I decided that I needed to test the waters, see how things really lay between us and whether we could begin to go back to the way things used to be. So the next day, when I saw her by herself between classes, I made my way over to her. It was important that I spoke to her when she was alone so that I could get to the real Lydia, not the one who couldn't lose face in front of her mates.

'Hi,' I said.

Not very original, I know, but I reckoned I could pretty much judge how she was going to be by her response to this one word. If she didn't want anything to do with me, she would either ignore it or sneer at me. On the other hand, if she did think that we had something worth salvaging, she might smile and say hi back.

And that's what she did.

I was a bit stuck then. I hadn't really thought much further than the initial contact, so I stuck with convention.

'How are you?'

'Fine, thanks. You?'

'Yeah, fine.'

This was all very well, but if I wasn't careful, the moment was going to pass, and all we would have established was that we were both healthy. My words came out all of a tumble when I spoke next.

'Look, Lydia, I'm really sorry that we fell out. Everything just got out of hand really quickly. I didn't mean to get you in trouble with your mum. I didn't even know that my mum had rung yours until you told me. It was all just a silly misunderstanding. Can't we just be friends again, like we were? I miss you.'

I realised that in my effort to start a conversation with her, I was gabbling. I bit my lip and waited for her to speak.

Lydia looked at me for a long time. I couldn't tell from her expression what she was thinking, and I felt a bit stupid just waiting. Then, just when I was going to tell her to forget the whole thing, and walk away, she came up close and threw her arms around my neck.

'I've missed you too.'

I felt the relief flood through my body. My life just hadn't been the same without Lydia in it. We didn't really need to say anything else. I knew in that moment that everything that had gone wrong over the last few weeks was forgotten and that we would be back to where we had been before Kyle's party.

Well, almost. There was still the sticky issue of our mums to consider. I didn't know exactly what my mum had said to Lydia's or what had been said back, but I was pretty sure that my mum wouldn't be exactly delighted that we were friends again. Still, we could cross that bridge when we came to it. Also, there was still one tiny, niggling doubt at the back of my head. The argument had all been Lydia's doing, even if she was being egged on by her mum. Lydia had been very quick to chuck the blame at me and to take all those giggling girls with her. Somewhere there was a little voice telling me to be careful, that if she'd done it once, she could do it all over again. Wasn't that what Juju had said too? I would have to tread cautiously.

That said, a couple of days later, I found myself in the cafe on Church Street telling Lydia all about Sam. She knew that I was still in contact with Juju – she'd seen the phone in my bag that time. So I told her about the shopping trips and the make-up and everything. Then I had to warn her that I'd had to tell Mum that it was hers. She pulled a bit of a face at that, but she could see that it had been a necessary lie.

'So have you told your mum now?' she asked. 'Is she OK with it?'

'No. I nearly did, and then somehow it didn't feel right. I will tell her but I just want to make sure of my ground with Juju first.'

'So where does she think you are every Saturday afternoon? You surely can't have been saying that you're at my house, not after "the row"!'

So I told her about the school play and how Mum thought

I was a dancer and that I was needed every Saturday for rehearsals. Lydia's eyes lit up with a new kind of respect for me that I'd never seen before.

'Genius!' she said approvingly.

I didn't tell her about the champagne afternoon, but I told her most of what Juju had said about Sam. Lydia was open-mouthed.

'So this Sam guy, the bloke from the news, he knew that she was pregnant, and basically told her she had to get rid of the baby? That's grim. What a rat! And that's why she had to give you up for adoption and everything?'

I nodded. It all seemed a bit strange talking about this baby who actually turned out to be me. Even though I was angry with Sam for not wanting anything to do with me, I knew that if Juju hadn't had me adopted, I would never have had Mum. Or Dad, for that matter. That was too weird to think about, so I tried not to.

'Do you want to meet him?' Lydia asked. 'You know, to confront him? Find out what he has to say for himself?'

I'd thought hard about this, and the truth was I just didn't know. I was cross that he'd abandoned Juju, but also I was kind of curious to meet him because he was almost a household name. I couldn't really see how having it out with him would make things any better though, and it could actually make things a whole load worse.

'I do and I don't,' I said slowly. 'Part of me would like to let him know that I exist, but if I do go and talk to him, it might all backfire in my face, and I'm not sure I could cope with that.'

As I could have predicted, Lydia was all for a huge showdown.

'If I were you,' she said, her eyes shining with the drama of it all, 'I would march down to the BBC and camp out there until

164

he came to talk to me. I'd make a scene and not be fobbed off until he explained himself.'

I smiled but I didn't really say anything else. Neither did Juju when I told her what Lydia had suggested, but I could see that her mind was going over all the possibilities. When I told her that Lydia and I had made up, she seemed a bit nervous that I had shared so much with her, but then I explained that Lydia was good with secrets. Even when we'd fallen out, she'd not breathed a word about Juju to anyone.

'Lydia said that it was really horrible what Sam did to you.' I continued. 'She said it doesn't seem right that he should go through his whole life not knowing what a mess you made of yours.'

I put my hand to my mouth. That came out all wrong. From where I was sitting, Juju's life looked incredibly successful. Luckily, she didn't seem to take offence. In fact, I wasn't sure that she was listening to me at all.

The afternoon continued as normal. We had popped out for ice cream, and I was just thinking about heading back to the tube station, when Juju went all serious on me.

'Just sit down a minute, Kitty,' she said.

I did as I was told. Juju bit her lip and fiddled with her blonde hair as she spoke, twisting it round her manicured finger.

'I've been wondering about what you said,' she said thoughtfully, a crease appearing between her grey eyes. 'Well, what Lydia said actually. Maybe you should go and see Sam?'

I was a bit taken aback. I didn't think she would like the idea one little bit. She'd told me before that she didn't want anything to do with Sam ever again. It seemed strange that, all of a sudden, she would want to throw me right into his path. So I just listened to her plan.

'You could do just what Lydia said, go to the BBC and get him to come and talk to you. I haven't got an address for him, and you won't be able to find him as easily as you found me, because people in the public eye protect their personal details so carefully. So ...'

She tapped her lips with her fingers, thinking out loud.

'You'd have to go to reception, tell them that you're Sam Cunningham's daughter and wait for him to come down.'

She seemed to be planning it all out in her head, and she spoke slowly as she pieced it together.

'Then you can tell him all about you and me and what he did, and ask him for an explanation.'

This struck me as a terrible idea. It was one thing confronting my birth dad about his dastardly deeds, but it was something else doing it in front of an audience. Mum always told me not to wash my dirty knickers in public. Until this moment, I'd never been quite sure what she meant, but now I did. I looked at Juju, assuming she would see by herself what a bad plan this was, but she was nodding as it all fell into place in her head. Maybe I was being silly, but it just felt wrong.

'Wouldn't it be a bit public, in reception?' I said in a last attempt to talk her out of it.

Juju didn't think so. She shook her head, and her eyes opened really wide.

'No,' she said. 'In reception would be perfect. Then he'll have to sit up and take notice. After all, he's in the public eye. He has something to protect. And he won't be able to just send you away in case you make a fuss in front of everyone.'

There was a glint in her eye that I hadn't seen before. I wasn't entirely sure I liked it.

'But when will I go? He works during the day and I'm at

school then.'

'Then you'll just have to bunk off,' she said. 'It'll be an adventure!'

Chapter 25

Pretending that I was at school on a Saturday was one thing. Bunking off during the week was quite another. I still wasn't convinced that it was a good idea, but it appeared that I was the only one with doubts. I had Lydia on one side and Juju on the other, both urging me on.

'I'll cover for you,' said Lydia confidently when we were talking about how I could make my grand escape work. It was break, and we had taken ourselves off to a quiet spot near the caretaker's office. Things were nearly back to normal between us, and the Bell twins seemed to have sloped out of our lives to irritate someone else. It was almost as if the row had never happened.

'I'll just say you're ill,' she said as if this would make all the difference in the world.

'Well, that won't work,' I said. 'Mum has to ring the school office and tell them. Otherwise, they'll ring her to find out where I am.'

'Hmmm,' said Lydia, and then she went quiet for a moment. She kicked her shoe against the wall as she thought, and I could see the smooth leather of the toecap scuffing. Mum would kill me if I did that to my shoes.

'Well,' she said after she'd had a think. 'Your mum can ring school and tell them that you're ill.'

'Don't be daft,' I said. 'Mum's got some kind of sickness radar. She can spot me faking at forty paces.'

'Not that mum,' said Lydia with a huge smile on her face, and suddenly I could see where she was coming from.

'You mean Juju could ring school? Sneaky.'

I turned the idea over in my mind, looking for flaws.

'Juju could ring to say that I was sick. I could go and see Sam, and as long as I was back before Mum got home from work, then she need never know.'

'Precisely,' said Lydia. 'I'm a genius.'

She did a bow and a little spin on the spot. You couldn't help loving Lydia, even after everything.

I still wasn't sure though. I didn't like lying to anyone – not even school. I know I'd been lying to Mum for ages but that was different. I just hadn't got round to telling her the truth. But lying to school? That felt bad. The trouble was, I couldn't see any other solution unless we could get hold of a home address for Sam, and the BBC were hardly going to give that out to me, even if I did tell them that I was his long-lost daughter.

Anyway, despite my doubts, a plan was hatched. Juju would ring school and tell them that I was ill and wouldn't be in. I would then make my way to the BBC building. It wasn't far from Juju's apartment, so it shouldn't be that difficult to find. Once I was there, I would just go in and ask for Sam Cunningham. What I'd do when he appeared, I wasn't entirely sure, but Juju seemed so convinced that it was a good idea that it got harder and harder to back out.

We decided to go for it on the Thursday. I got up as usual and dressed for school. As I left, I gave Mum a kiss on the cheek. She held on to me by the elbow.

'Are you alright?' she asked, her enquiring eyes scanning my face. I tell you, nothing gets past my mum.

'I'm fine,' I said, even though I was far from it.

'No more problems with Lydia?' she asked. 'Is she being mean again?'

'No, Mum. Lydia and me have made up.'

I saw a flicker of disappointment in her eyes.

'Honestly, I'm fine,' I said again. 'I'll see you tonight. I think there's a rehearsal after school, so I might be a bit late,' I added.

I didn't know how long this was all going to take, and I needed to get an excuse in ready.

'OK. Well, if you're sure,' said Mum doubtfully. 'Have a lovely day,' and she kissed me on the cheek carefully so that her lipstick didn't rub off on me.

As I was saying goodbye to Mum, Juju was ringing the school to tell them I'd been sick in the night and wouldn't be in school. I headed for the train station. I still had my uniform on, but I didn't want to have to carry it around with me all day, and anyway, I thought they might take me a bit more seriously at the BBC if I looked like a schoolgirl.

The journey ran smoothly, although the trains were really full of commuters and the compartments smelled of hot bodies and aftershave.

As I approached the BBC building, it looked absolutely massive, rising up from the street like some kind of palace. I looked up at it and felt my chest go tight and my heart race. What if he wasn't there after all this? What if he was but he was really horrible to me? But I couldn't back out now, not when I'd come so far. I'd be letting Juju down and I couldn't bear that.

I took a deep breath and made my way up the stone steps

to the front door and into the reception. It was huge and I suddenly felt very small. The ceiling was so high up that it reminded me a bit of a cathedral, but it wasn't made of stone. It was all glass and shiny silver pipes. I almost turned round there and then, but I stabbed my nails into my palms to give me strength and took a deep breath.

At the far end of the hall was a big white desk and some comfy leather chairs. I walked across to it as bravely as I could, my school shoes squeaking on the white tiled floor. The woman on the desk was busy looking at something on her computer screen, and she didn't look up as I approached. I didn't know what to do. It seemed rude to clear my throat, so I just stood there and waited for her to notice me. She didn't. I seemed to have been waiting for an age. I was just thinking that I might have to make some noise, when a tall man with lots of dark curly hair and who looked vaguely familiar came and stood next to me. Something about his movement must have caught the woman's eye, and at last she looked up.

'Ah, Mr Davies. How are you? What can I do for you?'

'Actually, I think this young lady needs your attention first,' he said, and gestured to me.

This was a nightmare. Now not only did I have to tell her what I wanted, but I had to do it with an audience of someone that I thought might actually be famous. I opened my mouth but no sound came out. The woman and the man both looked at me patiently, although she looked slightly less patient than him. I blushed and tried again.

'I was wanting to speak to Mr Sam Cunningham, please,' I said.

My voice sounded very small and quiet, but I couldn't seem to make it any louder.

'Do you have an appointment?' the woman asked.

She seemed to be speaking more quietly too. It must have been catching.

An appointment? That never even occurred to me and I started to panic. After all this effort, the plan was going to go wrong before it had even had a chance to get started.

'No,' I said.

If I spoke any quieter, my voice would disappear entirely.

'I didn't know that I needed one.'

I could feel tears starting to sting in my eyes. I wished the curly-haired man would just get on with whatever he was here to do.

'Well, not necessarily,' said the reception woman briskly. 'What do you want to see him about?'

'Is he here, then?' I asked, feeling a little bit brighter. At least that was a start.

'Yes, Mr Cunningham is here as far as I'm aware. And you wanted to see him because …?'

'It's kind of personal,' I muttered.

'Hmmm,' said the woman in a disapproving tone. 'Well, I can ring upstairs and see if he's prepared to spare you a moment. Who shall I say is here?'

It took me a while to realise that she was asking me what my name was.

'Well?' she prompted.

Giving her my name would mean nothing. He would have no idea who Kitty Cooper was. Why should he? I could tell her that I was his daughter, but what if he had a family of his own? This woman might know that he didn't have a daughter that looked like me. Then suddenly from nowhere, the solution came to me.

'Julia Boniface,' I said.

The woman was on the phone.

'Mr Cunningham, there's a young lady in reception asking to see you. Her name is Julia Boniface. Shall I tell her you'll come down?'

I stared at the woman, willing Sam to say he'd come. I think my heart stopped beating whilst I waited to hear what he'd said. She put the phone down and stared straight at me.

'He says he'll be down shortly. You can wait over there.'

She pointed at the leather chairs.

'Now, Mr Davies. Thank you for waiting. How may I help you?'

She was all smiles with him, I noticed.

I walked away from the desk towards the chairs. I sat down on the first one that I came to, but I perched right on the edge of it so that I could leap back up at a moment's notice if I had to. It was very busy in the hall, with people coming and going all the time, most of them without having to speak to the snooty receptionist. I could see that the lifts were over on the opposite side, so I kept my eyes on the doors.

My palms felt really clammy, and my breath was coming in little short bursts. I had been over what I wanted to say to him in my head so many times, but now that the moment was almost here, my mind was completely blank. All I could feel were nerves and a kind of deep-down rage. I hadn't really noticed how angry I was before. I was angry that this man had so abused my mother. I was angry that I had been robbed of a lifetime with Juju. I was angry that my dad had died, even though if it hadn't been for Sam, he wouldn't have been my Dad. But most of all, I was angry about how unfair the whole thing was. I hadn't noticed that I'd bunched my fists into little cannon balls until my forearms began to ache.

I must have waited there for five, ten minutes with no sign of him. I almost started to forget what I was doing there. I know that sounds funny, but my mind began wandering as I watched all the people coming and going, and wondered what they were all doing. There's something kind of strange being in that building, because famous people walk in all the time and no one bats an eyelid. There's a kind of a buzz about the place, and it was great just sitting there soaking it all up.

Anyway, I was just thinking about whether I would like to work there one day, when I realised that the lift had been and gone, and I hadn't noticed who had got out of it. Quickly I jerked my gaze back to the doors, and there he was. He looked smaller than he did on the telly, which was weird because obviously he was much bigger than when he was in the box in the corner of my lounge. His hair was all over the place as if he'd had his hands in it, and he had on his little round glasses. He was looking around all over the place, which seemed a bit odd until I realised that he would be looking for Juju. Not seeing anyone who could possibly be her, even allowing for the thirteen years since he'd last seen her, he went to check with the woman on reception. I saw her nod her head towards me, and suddenly I felt really, incredibly shy.

When he realised that I was a child in school uniform, Sam seemed to relax. He grew a little taller and his shoulders dropped. Then he walked over to me. I could see that he was curious though. He wasn't smiling at me but he wasn't exactly frowning either. When he got close enough, he stuck out his right hand as if he wanted to shake mine. It was such an alien gesture to me, but almost as a reflex, I stuck mine out too. I didn't stand up though, so he had to bend down quite a long way to reach me.

'Julia?' he asked. His voice was gentler than it was on his news reports.

Suddenly I didn't feel nervous at all. The anger that had been bubbling up inside me ever since Juju had told me what he had done was so close to the surface that all you would have to do was touch me and it would all have come exploding out. I stood up as tall as I could stand.

'My name is Kitty Rose Cooper,' I spat.

'Well, why did you call yourself Julia?' he asked gently.

'Because I wanted to make sure you'd come. And it worked, didn't it?'

Even I could hear the note of triumph in my voice.

'I used to know someone called Julia Boniface,' he said. 'But you seem to know that already. What I want to know now is who you are and why you've come to see me.'

His voice was really calm, and it was making it difficult for me to sustain my anger, but I was determined to show him just what I thought of him. I started my speech clearly and loudly.

'She's my mother. Well, my birth mother. I'm the baby that you wanted aborted thirteen years ago. You're my dad.'

People must have been turning round to stare at us – I was making a lot of noise – but I just didn't care who was watching. I just carried on with my speech, my voice getting louder still.

'You told her to get rid of me and she didn't, and then she had to give me away because she was too young to look after me properly, and it broke her heart. And she couldn't go to university and it was all your fault, but you still went to Bristol and got your degree and everything. I bet you didn't give her a second's thought, did you?'

I was shouting now. It almost hurt my throat and I'd started to cry. I didn't mean to but I just couldn't help it. Tears raced down my cheeks.

'Hang on, sorry, what did you say your name was? Kitty, wasn't it? Hang on, Kitty. Let's stop shouting and calm down a little bit.'

He moved round the chairs until he was at the one next to mine, and then he sat down and gestured for me to do the same. Suddenly I felt as if all my strength had evaporated. I collapsed onto the seat.

'Now, let's get this all sorted out.'

He was talking to me in this really gentle way, and I started to feel a little bit less angry.

'Obviously, this is all news to me,' he said. 'As far as I knew, Juju, your mother, your birth mother, had chosen to have an abortion. I had no idea that she'd had the baby, you. I haven't seen her since she left the school that we were at. I tried to find out where she'd gone, but her mother was so angry with me that she wouldn't give me an address or anything. I had no idea that you existed, Kitty. If I had done …'

'Oh, how very touching,' said someone behind me.

It was a harsh, bitter voice that I didn't recognise, and when I turned to see where it was coming from, there was Juju. She looked amazing. She was wearing a tight black sleeveless dress with a red silk scarf knotted at her neck and the highest high heels I'd ever seen anyone wear. I was so relieved to see her. I'd thought I was going to have to deal with this all by myself, but now she had arrived, it meant that everything was going to be alright. I smiled at her to show her how pleased I was to see her, but she didn't smile back. She just looked at me as if I was something that smelled really bad.

'Look at this,' she sneered. 'Daddy and daughter reunion.

How lovely. Well, I suppose it's not actually a reunion, is it?' she corrected herself. 'Seeing as you didn't know anything about your darling little baby, did you, Sam? Can I see any family resemblance, I wonder?'

She looked from me to Sam and back again, but her grey eyes, my eyes, were cold.

'Well, only if you count a tendency to snivel. You used to do a fair bit of that, didn't you, Sam darling? You certainly snivelled the night I told you that I was going to abort your child. You should have heard him, sweet pea. Begging me, he was, begging me to have his precious little offspring and not kill it.'

I was shocked. This wasn't how she'd explained it all to me – not a bit. As far as I knew, it was the other way around. Sam had made her have the abortion. That's what she'd said. It was Juju who hadn't been able to go through with it and had me adopted. I was about to say something, object to this new version of events, when Juju cut across me and continued.

'It was alright for you though, wasn't it, Sammy Boy? You had your shining career ahead of you. All those high expectations to match up to, whereas I was going nowhere.'

I was really confused. It was all getting muddled in my head.

'But I thought you were going to go to Bath,' I said. 'So you could be near him when he was at Bristol. You had it all planned out. That's what you said.'

I looked at her, hoping for some sort of clarification. I wanted her to stop talking like this. This wasn't how it was meant to go at all. This wasn't what we agreed, what I'd agreed.

'Oh, don't be so naive, Kitty darling,' Juju said, her lip turning up in a sneer. 'There was no way I would ever have got the grades to go to university. Secretarial college. That was what

177

they had in mind for me. But golden boy here. He was a straight-A kind of student. No darkness on his horizon.'

'Can we talk about this somewhere less public?' Sam asked, and tried to move Juju towards an office just off the hall, but Juju stood her ground.

'Oh, you'd like that, wouldn't you, Sammy Boy? Hush it up. Brush it all under the carpet. Well, I've been quiet for far too long. Over here boys!'

She turned around and I saw a little troop of photographers coming across the reception hall towards us.

'Come and get your snaps. Mr "Big Shot" Sam Cunningham and his little long-lost love-child.'

Suddenly there were flashes going off everywhere. It took me a moment to work out what was happening. Then two huge security guards appeared from somewhere and started to try and move the photographers back the way they had come. Juju and Sam were standing almost nose to nose, shouting at each other. I didn't know what to do, so I just ran.

Chapter 26

I didn't know where I was going. I flew out of the building and out onto the pavement. The street was busy but I shoved my way through the crowds so that I could get as far away as possible. People were shouting after me as I slammed into them, but I didn't care who I pushed. I just had to leave it all behind me.

I felt humiliated and embarrassed, but most of all I felt hurt. How could Juju have done that to me? I thought she was supposed to care. She'd been kind to me, bought me things, welcomed me into her life. I couldn't believe that it had all been a lie. Not right from the start.

I remembered how she was when she told me the story of her and Sam. She'd seemed really upset. She'd cried and everything, but she'd just been feeding me a line, and I took the bait. Hook, line and sinker. She'd encouraged me to confront Sam, and all the time, she just wanted to … Well, what exactly? Humiliate him as well?

I thought about all the photographers. They hadn't been there by coincidence. She must have set the whole thing up just to embarrass him. Or for the money? Of course. The papers would pay her for her story. That's when it struck me how cleverly I'd been played. She hadn't cared about me at all. She'd just used me to get at Sam. I wondered how much cash she'd been promised. Sam was a household name. There would have been loads of interest in the story, especially with all those photos. My heart sank again as I ran. I'd been so stupid.

After a while I just didn't have the strength to run any further. There was a park in front of me. It must have been Regent's Park. I made for the gate and looked for somewhere to sit away from everybody. There was a bench set back a bit from the path and I made for it. As I sat down, I noticed the brass plaque on it: 'For Christina, who loved this place.'

I wondered who Christina was and whether her life was as much of a mess as mine. I don't know how long I sat there for. People passed me, hurrying through the park as a shortcut or walking their dogs. Women with pushchairs gathered in groups, and joggers ran by with their headphone cables flapping. I just sat and thought and cried a bit. I didn't know what to do next. I didn't really know where I was even, although it wouldn't have been that difficult to find my way back to St Pancras and catch the train to Woodston. Somehow I just didn't have the strength for it. I needed someone to pick me up and brush me down and give me a hug and tell me that everything would be alright. I needed Mum.

It didn't cross my mind that I shouldn't ring her at work or how much trouble I'd be in when she found out about all the lies I'd told her. I just dialled the number and waited whilst it rang.

'Kitty? Is everything alright? You're not supposed to ring me when I'm at work, you know.'

She sounded more put out than angry.

'Mum?' I managed.

'What is it? What's the matter?'

Mum knew me so well. She could tell just from my one word that something was very wrong. I could feel the tears starting to fill my eyes again.

'Oh, Mum,' I said. 'I've made such a mess of everything.'

I started to cry again and my breath came in huge gulping sobs.

'Kitty! What on earth is the matter? Where are you?'

'I'm in Regent's Park, I think.'

There was a pause.

'What? What on earth are you doing there? Why aren't you at school? Are you safe? Are you hurt? Has someone hurt you?'

Mum's questions came so quickly that I didn't even try to answer them but just let them wash over me.

'I'm OK. I'm not hurt. Can you come? Can you come and get me? Please.'

Mum arrived about an hour later. By that time, the afternoon was wearing on, and primary school children had arrived on bikes and scooters to race around in the sunshine. She was running towards my bench. She looked older, almost wild with worry, and when she saw me, she began to run faster than I've ever seen her move in my whole life. And I ran too. I ran towards my mum and threw my arms around her neck.

'Mum,' I cried. 'I'm so sorry. I'm so very sorry.'

Then we sat on Christina's bench and I told her everything, right from the start. I told her how Lydia and I had thought she might need some help and how I'd been in her black box file.

'I knew,' she said. 'I knew you must have been in it. Things weren't in the right order. I had no idea what you wanted it for though. Oh, Kitty. That's why I was in your wardrobe that time. I was looking for clues.'

Then I told her how I'd found Juju's name and then her address and arranged to meet her.

'And you went all the way across town by yourself to meet a complete stranger. Oh, Kitty! Anything could have happened to you. What were you thinking?'

She stroked my mousy hair as I talked but she didn't look cross or anything.

Then I told her about the phone and the make-up and how Juju had told me about Sam and how we had worked out a way for me to confront him. Mum looked more and more worried as the story all came spilling out of me, and every so often she would make me stop whilst she questioned me on something specific.

'So you haven't been at rehearsals on a Saturday?'

I felt dreadful. All my lies were all tumbling out one on top of another. I shook my head guiltily.

'Well, I was really looking forward to seeing you in that show!'

She gave me a half smile and I knew everything was going to be alright.

'Oh, Kitty. Princess. What a mess. Why didn't you just tell me what you were doing?'

'I'm so sorry, Mum. I really am. I hated lying to you. It's been so awful.'

Then I burst into tears again and Mum put her arms around me and held me safe. We just sat there for ages, hugging on Christina's bench.

Chapter 27

So that's it, my story.

The next day, the tabloid papers were full of it. The headlines read 'Top BBC Reporter in Call Girl Scandal'.

That was when it finally dawned on me how Juju made a living. I couldn't believe that it hadn't occurred to me before. I remembered the man leaving the apartment the day I'd got there early, and the two champagne glasses the day she was drunk. Fortunately, there didn't seem to be much mention of me in the story. My name wasn't in the paper. Mum said the lawyers at the BBC must have kept me out of it, and I wasn't in the photo that was on the front page either. There they were, my birth parents, nose to nose. Juju had her finger pointed at Sam as if she was going to try to gouge his eyes out, and Sam's hand was up as if he was asking her to calm down. It was awful and Mum wouldn't have a copy of it in the flat.

I never heard from Juju again. Mum took the phone that she'd bought from me and threw it down the loo so that it wouldn't work. Then she made me get a new SIM card so that

I had a totally new phone number. It was a bit of a pain letting everyone know, but it meant that Juju couldn't contact me. I didn't mind. I didn't want to see her ever again.

I felt a bit bad about Sam though. I had given him a hard time when he didn't deserve it. I sent him a card at Christmas, care of the BBC. I checked with Mum first – I've learned my lesson on that score – and we put our address in it.

He wrote back, and a couple of weeks later, Mum and I met him for dinner. He took us for a burger. It was nice. He's a nice guy – not as nice as Dad was, but not bad really. I think I'll keep in touch with him, not as my dad or anything like that. More as a kind of friend.

When Sam tells me about his work, it sounds really exciting. I quite fancy being a journalist when I leave school. I wouldn't mind working on a newspaper – a broadsheet, not one of those rags that Juju sold her story, our story, to. After all, being a journalist is all about discovering secrets and telling stories, and I'm quite good at that!

Please Leave a Review

If you have enjoyed this book then I would really appreciate it if you would leave a review on Amazon and Goodreads. Social proof is vital to independent authors and it helps other people who might enjoy my books to find them. Thank you.

About the Author

Lucinda Fox writes fast-paced stories for girls from 11 to 15. She lives in Yorkshire, England with her husband and children.

Her first burning ambition was to be a solicitor and so she read Law at Manchester University and then worked for many years at a commercial law firm.

After leaving her legal career behind to care for her children, Lucinda turned to her second love - books. She returned to university, studying part-time whilst the children were at school and was awarded a BA in English Literature with First Class Honours.

Lucinda loves sunshine, travel, the sea, bluebells and pancakes drizzled with maple syrup.

She also writes women's contemporary fiction as Imogen Clark.

Also by Lucinda Fox

The Fame Game

Do you dream of being rich and famous?

Teenager Lydia Tench wants a piece of the glamorous celebrity lifestyle that she sees in magazines so when her family volunteers to take part in a reality TV show she is certain that it will catapult her straight into the spotlight. But it turns out that finding fame is not as straight-forward as Lydia hopes…

The Fame Game by Lucinda Fox is the second in the Kitty Cooper series of books for young teenage girls. If you like fast-paced tales of life as a teenager then this book is for you.

Buy The Fame Game today and join Kitty and Lydia on their latest entertaining adventure.

The Dream Team

What if the boy you fancy doesn't even know you exist?

When Lydia falls for the gorgeous star of the school football team her best friend Kitty decides that they need to get fit to get noticed. It looks like their plan is working when they land places on the school netball squad but one of the team members has other ideas. Tired of Keisha's nastiness, Lydia comes up with a challenge that will decide who is the best once and for all. But can she actually win?'

Dream Team by Lucinda Fox is the third in the Kitty Cooper series of books for young teenage girls. If you like fast-paced tales of teenage life then this book is for you.

Pick up The Dream Team today and join Kitty and Lydia on their most dangerous adventure yet.

Printed in Great Britain
by Amazon

42806069R00116